PRAISE FOR
THE BOOKS OF TONY MENDOZA

Los Angeles Times, **Sunday March 12, 2000**
(Cuba: Going Back)

"In his brilliant photographs, Mendoza doesn't betray any interest in the exile fantasies of return. He teases us, plays with our love of nostalgia, by bathing his black and white prints in sepia, making them look older...but, through his lens, Mendoza shows us the present disintegrating: An elderly man earns a few pesos filling cigarette lighters; the police checks a taxi driver's papers; a small boy plays baseball in the rubble; a sickly dog searches for scraps of food. What the gifted Mendoza delivers is the topography of a wasteland."

Camerawork, **Spring/Summer 2000**
(Cuba: Going Back)

"Mendoza's book, with it's strong textual emphasis on political and social reform, reads like an updated and refined version of *How the Other Half Lives (by Jacob Riis.)*"

Miami Herald, **December 26, 1999**
(Cuba: Going Back)

"A subtle yet striking collection of sepia-like photographs depicting life in Cuba, coupled with the perceptive observations of a Cuban exile returning home for the first time in 36 years, make this more than a coffee table dust-catcher...The result is a fascinating and even-handed book, yet sometimes harshly critical, word-and-picture view. While the information gathered and the pictures taken date to 1996, events of the intervening three years have done little to alter this volume's timeliness. In fact, it may be even more relevant now. "

A Cuban Summer

TONY MENDOZA

A Cuban Summer

a novel

2013 · CAPRA PRESS, SAN FRANCISCO

ISBN: 978-1-59266-102-2

Library of Congress Control Number: 2013942086

Book design & typography:
Studio E Books, Santa Barbara, California

Cover wave photo:
Tony Mendoza

Published by Capra Press
San Francisco, California
http://caprapress.net

*This book is dedicated to
the Cuba before Fidel that I remember
with affection, a country that overflowed with
energy, laughter, and many imperfections.*

A Cuban Summer

1

TONY DE LA TORRE DIDN'T KNOW
when it began. Maybe when he was twelve, maybe eleven-and-a-half. But in the spring of 1954, at thirteen, his transformation was complete. He lusted after every female who crossed his path.

He assumed that his ever-present stream of sexual fantasies was nature at work, possibly intensified by Havana, a city where he knew he could buy sex as easily as he bought a cup of coffee. He also assumed it was normal for boys his age to masturbate. He did it, and all the boys he knew did it. But this habit presented a problem. He went to Belén, the largest Jesuit school in Havana, and the school required that all boys go to confession once a week. He tried to stay away from the details of his errant behavior by reciting, very fast, his chronic recurring infractions:

"Father, I lied, I had bad thoughts, I masturbated."

Masturbation was the one sin that truly bothered the priests, yet he had no intention of stopping. He couldn't fall asleep if he did not do it at night, and he couldn't get out of bed before doing it in the morning. He also did it in the afternoon, after school, while taking a bath.

He suspected his habit was excessive.

"My son, how many times did you masturbate during the week?"

"Twenty-one times, Father."

Tony heard a long, heavy sigh.

"My son, your behavior is unacceptable. Don't you understand that every time you masturbate the devil is clamping a stronger hold on you? Don't you understand that if you die after you masturbate, you go to hell for an eternity?"

"Yes, Father," Tony replied, even though it didn't seem fair that a pleasure measured in seconds should be punishable with pain and torture for an eternity. Before assigning the penance, the priest asked:

"Are you going to try to stop this disgraceful and dangerous weakness?"

"Yes, Father," Tony said, committing the first lie for his next confession.

Then he discovered Father Zulueta. He decided to try him when he noticed that the line to Father Zulueta's confessional was always the longest line and soon learned why.

Unlike the other priests, Father Zulueta was not interested in the frequency of masturbation. Tony recited his list and Father Zulueta simply said:

"Try to be better."

That was it.

Father Zulueta was resigned to the ways of Cuban boys. He gave short penances. Often, he ended the confession by saying:

"Pray for me. I'm also flesh."

That was a clear signal that Father Zulueta also masturbated. He was a flawed priest, and Tony liked him for it. He was also thankful that Father Zulueta never pursued the "I had bad thoughts" part of his confession. That confession would have been embarrassing if he had had to describe his bad thoughts.

2

TONY HAD BAD THOUGHTS EVERY time he stepped out of his front gates and headed uphill to 23rd Street, the main commercial avenue in the Vedado district of Havana. 23rd Street was only one block away from his house and was usually overflowing with attractive females. He could watch them walking toward him, walking in front of him, crossing the streets, walking out of restaurants, waiting for the trolley, and working the coffee stands. His propensity for bad thoughts went into high gear on that avenue.

There was a coffee stand on every corner of 23rd Street, and the popularity of each stand depended on the attractiveness of the female operator. His favorite coffee stand was on 23rd and J, two blocks from his house.

A large group of men collected there at all hours. They argued about baseball or politics, they smoked cigars, and they flirted with the operator. The young woman who ran that coffee machine was as attractive as a movie star, in Tony's opinion. He often went to the coffee stand after school and asked her for a *cortadito*, a small cup of espresso. What he especially liked about her was how she always referred to her clients as *mi amor*, or *mi vida*, my life. She seemed to be on intimate terms with everyone. When Tony ordered his *cortadito* she often said: *como estás, mi amorcito?* How are you, my little love? It was worth getting a cup of coffee at that stand just to hear her say that.

Gonzalo, his family's chauffeur, claimed that working girls were the sexiest. They worked to afford their own apartments so that they could get away from their families and the old traditions, like going out on a date with a chaperone or waiting for marriage to have sex. They wanted to be modern and free. In one of Tony's favorite fantasies, the coffee operator at 23rd and J would lean close to him and whisper: "*Mi amorcito*, why don't you come to my apartment when I'm done? I'll make you some good homebrewed coffee."

Sylvia Machado inspired another bout of erotic fantasies every time she came to his house to play Canasta with his mother. Sylvia could have worked as Ava Gardner's double. She was divorced. In Cuban society, being divorced was as bad as having leprosy, but as far as Tony was concerned, it made Sylvia even more exciting and possibly available. He also assumed that after years of living a solitary divorced life, she now yearned for the touch of a man. Tony noticed how she always paid attention to him—how she greeted him with a big smile, as if he amused her, as if she was especially glad to see him.

Then she came closer and offered her cheek for Tony to kiss. She always smelled like jasmine. Tony could not help thinking how exciting it would be to continue kissing her and how lucky her ex-husband must have been when he was still married to her. The only way he could describe Sylvia's body: *Esta buenísima*. She is in a state of extreme goodness. Tony knew that Sylvia had been a champion swimmer for the Havana Yacht Club. He figured all that practice and exercise must have contributed to her excellent figure.

The divorce was undoubtedly her ex-husband's fault. He probably got caught doing it with one of the maids. What an idiot! Had Tony been her husband, he would have been a model husband, religiously faithful and very focused on pleasing Sylvia. Being married to Sylvia had to be the equivalent of winning the lottery. He also would not have slept one wink during their entire marriage. Tony saw her the previous summer on Varadero Beach, in a tight and very sexy one-piece bathing suit. That image stayed with him for a long time, and at night, in his bed, he stared at the ceiling concocting improbable situations all ending with him and Sylvia in bed, in a passionate and amorous embrace.

Then there was Lucia. She was the youngest maid in his grandfather's house. His grandfather, Cocó Campos, had nine servants and most had been with him for years, like Rolando, the black cook from Oriente, who had been cooking for Cocó for thirty years. There was José Ignacio, the impeccably correct Spanish butler from Galicia, who immigrated to Cuba during the Spanish Civil War and had been with Cocó ever since. There was an assortment of maids, in their forties and fifties, who had also been around forever. Cocó paid his servants well, or well enough so that the turnover was minimal; but there seemed to be a revolving slot for a young maid, someone from a small town in one of the provinces. She would stay in the house for two or three years until she met a man who wanted to marry her, and then she'd be gone.

Gonzalo also had his eyes on Lucia. Gonzalo was in his middle thirties and married. But it seemed to Tony that Gonzalo's sexual appetite was insatiable.

Gonzalo had explained to him that provincial girls viewed sex as a natural, matter-of-fact activity because they were used to watching farm animals doing it and there was nothing else to do in the provinces besides working the land all day and having sex the rest of the time. In the provinces, Gonzalo claimed, sex was not viewed as a sin. It was viewed as nature. Tony knew that Gonzalo was prone to exaggerate, but his natural-girl-from-the-provinces theory made sense. He watched Lucia more closely after listening to Gonzalo. He watched her while she dusted around the house or mopped the marble floors, and noticed how the muscles in her arms flexed, so unlike the girls in his sister's group who had no muscles. Tony also enjoyed watching how her maid's uniform revealed a firm and generous figure.

Lucia noticed Tony watching her. Sometimes she answered his glances with a smile and a polite "good morning." She never said much more and neither did Tony.

In his Lucia fantasies, he knew what to do: every morning, after the adults left the house, he sneaked into his aunt's bedroom where Lucia was busy making the bed. The moment he entered the room, she smiled, told him to make sure the door was locked and then started to take off her clothes. Tony also undressed, then leaped onto the unmade bed doing a perfect somersault. Lucia laughed and joined him, then introduced him to all sorts of natural and matter-of-fact, country-style sexual activities.

Tony's fantasies were more or less on hold during his classes at Belén, while he concentrated on fractions, the eating habits of manatees, and the distinctions between Limbo and Purgatory. He managed to do all his homework in study halls at school. After school he took a bath, masturbated while coming up with sexual fantasies featuring Lucia, Sylvia Machado or Ava Gardner, and then retreated to his room where he listened to the latest *boleros* on the radio.

It seemed easy for him to get lost in the love songs.

Nosotros, a bolero by Pedro Junco, played constantly on Havana radios in the spring of 1954. The wonderful melody and the sorrowful mood of the song had a powerful effect on Tony. He memorized the lyrics:

> *We*
> *We were so sincere*
> *From the moment we met*
> *We have loved each other*
>
> *We*
> *We made our love*
> *A wonderful world*
> *A divine romance*
>
> *We*
> *Who love each other so much*
> *We must separate*
> *Don't ask me why anymore*
>
> *It's not because I don't love you*
> *I love you with all my heart*
> *I swear I adore you*
> *But in the name of this love*
> *And for your own good*
> *I must say goodbye*

He was surprised by the feelings of empathy and sadness that the songs evoked, as if the singer's story mirrored his own story. While he had not yet come close to having a girlfriend or experiencing love, he felt increasingly ready for both.

3

TONY ENJOYED GOING ON ERRANDS
with Gonzalo to Old Havana. Gonzalo was driving, as usual, like a
maniac. He tailgated, honked, cut in front of other drivers, yelled
at them, and swore at them. The other drivers were the enemy,
none of whom, according to Gonzalo, knew how to drive. At the
same time, he was always on the lookout for attractive female
pedestrians. He felt compelled, like many Cuban men, to say
something to attractive women walking on the sidewalk. Gonzalo
claimed it was his duty as a man to acknowledge female beauty.
When Tony's mother, or his grandmother, was on the car, Gonzalo
was the model of propriety. He drove slowly and carefully and did
not speak unless spoken to. His uniform—a gray suit, white shirt,
black tie, and a gray cap—was always pressed and clean.

But now Tony was the only passenger and Gonzalo was talking
nonstop, tie loose, cap off, honking the horn incessantly. Within

ten minutes he came to a screeching halt three times—every time because of a generously proportioned female sighting. Gonzalo was very clear about his aesthetics: large was beautiful, especially large behinds. He didn't care for slim women. Slim women, according to Gonzalo, were inadequate for sex.

Before they reached the seamstress' apartment in Old Havana, Gonzalo must have pulled alongside three or four curvaceous pedestrians and composed a different *piropo* for each. To a woman with a tight dress and a formidable behind he said: "Precious, I'll give my life to be reincarnated as your favorite chair."

She didn't even laugh.

To a pale young woman dressed in black: "I wonder who has died in heaven that has the angels in mourning." The angel in black laughed slightly, and Gonzalo was fast after her—offering her a ride, asking for her telephone number, but again, she ignored him.

Then, in the middle of a narrow Old Havana street, he spotted a woman that came close to his idea of physical perfection; a situation that called for a more dramatic effort. He stopped the car in the middle of the street, abandoned it, and walked fast to catch up with the attractive *mulata* whom he bombarded with a string of *piropos* until she smiled, his signal that she may be ready to give him her phone number.

In the meantime, growing numbers of furious drivers, stalled behind Tony's family's black Cadillac, were honking their horns. Gonzalo ignored them all and calmly went on with his business. When he got back to the car, he winked at Tony.

"I got her phone number!"

"I didn't see you write it down," Tony said, dubious of Gonzalo's claim.

"Don't worry. I never forget the number of a beautiful *mulata*."

When they got near the seamstress' address, Gonzalo parked

the car. He jumped out and returned five minutes later with his mother's dress. "I'm going to visit a friend on Obispo Street," he told Tony. "I'll be back in twenty minutes."

Gonzalo claimed he had a girlfriend in every sector of the city where he was sent on errands. Tony watched him walk away at such a quick pace that he assumed he was going to visit one of them. While he waited, Tony decided to go for a walk around Barrio Colón, a nearby neighborhood notorious for its large number of brothels.

It was near the end of the workday, and the sidewalks were overflowing with office workers heading home. The noise level in Old Havana streets was alarming. There was a continual traffic jam. Drivers took turns honking their horns, lottery vendors screamed their numbers, peanut vendors yelled: *maní, maní,* jackhammers hammered, jukeboxes in corner bars blared the latest *boleros* by Benny More and Celia Cruz, men whistled or made loud kissing noises directed at female pedestrians. Above the street, residents leaned on balcony railings and engaged in loud conversations with residents on the balconies across the street.

Tony observed men walking in and out of the brothels. He recognized brothels by the presence of women sitting behind the iron bars, guarding the windows, saying something to every man who passed by.

A group of boisterous and drunk American sailors, beer bottles in hand, passed by him. As he turned around to watch them, a woman extended both arms through the iron grills of her window and, like a Human Venus Flytrap, grabbed one of the sailors and pressed him against her window grill. She made her pitch.

Tony became more cautious by keeping a safe distance from the window grills. His hair bleached very light during the beach season and often he was mistaken for an American. A woman, sitting by a window, started talking to him, in very poor English:

"American boy, come here. We make good love. Two dollars."

"No, thank you," Tony said, very politely. He had no interest in ever going to a brothel in Barrio Colón. These were the cheapest brothels in Havana and were considered very low class. However, he liked being asked.

He kept walking and repeated his "no, thank you" after every new proposal, always trying to enunciate his English clearly. He liked posing as an American in Barrio Colón. He liked the deception, and he liked the attention. After a while, he looked at his watch and decided it was time to walk back to the car. He was sitting on the engine hood when Gonzalo showed up.

"I just did it with my girlfriend," Gonzalo announced, smiling broadly.

Tony never knew what to believe when Gonzalo talked about his sexual affairs. It could all be true. Gonzalo was handsome and simpatico. Everyone liked Gonzalo. But in this instance, Tony thought, there could not have been enough time for chivalry and romance since barely twenty minutes had passed before he returned to the car.

"You did it very fast," Tony observed.

"We did it on the living room floor," Gonzalo replied.

"Why?"

"Why not?" Gonzalo said, grinning.

As they drove home, Tony kept thinking about Gonzalo's brief report of his sexual activities. Maybe they did it on the living room floor because walking over to the bedroom involved wasting precious seconds. Maybe she did not do it in her bedroom because that bed was reserved for her husband. Maybe Gonzalo was lying, and he went someplace for a cup of coffee.

"I don't know Gonzalo," Tony said. "It doesn't sound too comfortable, doing it on the floor. I think it would be much more comfortable doing it on a bed."

"How would you know? You haven't done it anywhere. Let me ask you. When am I going to take you to a brothel?"

Gonzalo often asked Tony this question because in well-off Havana households, chauffeurs were entrusted with the sexual initiation of the oldest son. It was clearly Gonzalo's job to take Tony to a brothel. Fathers in Havana did not do that job—maybe because it was not considered in good taste—and there was always the possibility that one of the women would greet the father as one greets a regular customer. Tony didn't think that situation was likely to arise in his father's case; his father, Victor de la Torre, had a reputation to uphold. He was considered the top golfer and one of the best bridge players in Havana. He was perfectly happy playing those games, all day, every day at the Havana Country Club. Chasing after women was not part of his routine.

At thirteen, he was not overly interested in going to a brothel, but he didn't want to give the impression of being uninterested. He confessed to Gonzalo about his obsessive train of bad thoughts.

"Thinking is one thing," Gonzalo said, "but doing is another."

Gonzalo didn't think it was right for a thirteen-year-old boy to spend so much time making model planes or bouncing balls off walls. He wanted Tony to go to one of those brothels in Barrio Colón and get on with the business of being a man. He needed to be less a thinker and more a doer. If he didn't do it soon, he could turn into a *maricón*.

The way Gonzalo saw it, a thirteen-year-old Cuban boy who was still a virgin was headed in the wrong direction.

Tony knew that he had to go to a brothel soon. He not only had to contend with Gonzalo's nagging on a daily basis, but also with Ramiro, his first cousin his exact age, who had already gone to Marina, a popular three-dollar brothel named after its owner.

4

RAMIRO HAD ALWAYS BEEN HIS
best friend among his first cousins. They were born two days apart
in the same Havana hospital, and they grew up playing together. Lately, Ramiro was becoming unbearable. He never missed
a chance to kid Tony about his condition: "What's the matter,"
Ramiro often said, grinning. "Are you a mouse? Are you afraid to
go to Marina?"

Sure, he was afraid. He still felt more like a boy who made
model planes and bounced balls off walls than like a man who
drank at bars and went to brothels. As long as he could remember,
Ramiro specialized in being mindless, like breaking his arm three
times before he was nine: twice high up on a tree jumping unsuc-
cessfully for the same branch.

Ramiro's parents lived with his other grandfather, his de la

Torre grandfather, in a large house in the Country Club section of Havana, a residential area that was a good distance from the Vedado area where Tony lived. However, Tony still managed to see Ramiro on the weekends.

They met at the Havana Yacht Club, went snorkeling in the morning, and then ate lunch. After lunch, they took the trolley to get to the Miramar movie theater, four stops from the Yacht Club. Ramiro never went inside the trolley. Instead, he rode standing on the back fender, dangerously holding on and having to contend with both the policemen and the conductors. The tram cost only five *centavos*, so Tony chose to ride inside, usually in the back seat where he could keep an eye on his cousin on the fender.

At the movies, Ramiro's preferred seat was on the first row of the second floor balcony. He often brought a paper bag full of eggs. In the middle of the movie, he tossed the eggs, one at a time, into the darkness below. They would hear a splat and then a howl, as a horrified moviegoer discovered what had happened. Ramiro was a budding delinquent. It was impossible to keep up with Ramiro's current school because he had been kicked out of Belén, La Salle and all the other reputable schools in Havana. For the next school year, he was going to the Havana Military Academy, the only school that had the courage to take him.

Now Ramiro was claiming that he had gone to Marina and wanted Tony to go with him. Tony knew this: He had no interest in going there. Marina was one step above Barrio Colón, but he had heard that getting crabs was almost guaranteed if you did it at Marina.

If he decided to go to a brothel, he planned to go to the Mambo Club, where he could dance with the women before choosing one. He liked the idea of having a conversation before doing it. He had heard that the Mambo had a house doctor who inspected the staff every day. It was considered the classiest among Havana brothels; and at ten dollars, it was also one of the most expensive compared to three dollars at Marina.

Some of the women at the Mambo were reputed to be very attractive, and some were ex-chorus dancers from the Tropicana nightclub. Tony had heard that General Batista, who had recently installed himself as Cuba's dictator, went there. Batista called one hour ahead for the club to get rid of all their customers; the General wanted all the women for himself and his entourage. Tony was amused every time he imagined the entire Cuban cabinet running around naked, chasing the women in the Mambo Club.

Nevertheless, he was in no rush to go to the Mambo, mostly because the mechanics of lovemaking were still a mystery to him. He couldn't visualize how it was done. He knew that he didn't want to go to Marina with Ramiro, or go to any other brothel during the approaching summer vacation. There would be plenty of time in the future to do that.

After he turned thirteen, Tony was consciously trying not to do too many things with Ramiro. Ramiro was scary. His friends were even worse—all the confirmed juvenile delinquents at the Havana Yacht Club.

What most disturbed Tony about Ramiro and his friends was how frequently they got into fistfights. Starting a fistfight, especially for a silly inconsequential reason, was a test of manhood. They also swore often, another sign of manhood. And Cuban swearwords, when uttered by boys, were dangerous—they could break a nose. If a boy called Tony a *maricón* or a *hijo de puta*, the only honorable and manly response was to fight him. The solution for dealing with Ramiro and his friends was to avoid them. The only thing he planned to do with Ramiro, when the beach season at the Yacht Club started in early May, was snorkeling on Saturday mornings. He figured he could not get into too much trouble snorkeling with Ramiro.

Tony got to the Yacht Club early, changed into his bathing suit, and walked to the basketball courts where he expected to find his cousin shooting baskets. Ramiro wasn't there, so Tony thought he might be at the pool. The pool area was mostly empty, except for a small group of girls from his age group sunbathing on the deck chairs. He knew the girls, but he was not about to go up to them by himself and talk to them.

He decided to try the courts again, and halfway there he spotted Ramiro walking toward him. He was thinking that while it was easy for him to criticize Ramiro, he had to admit he also admired him. Ramiro was a very good athlete. He was amusing. Girls liked him.

Ramiro was a doer—he did crazy things. He was gutsy. In a way, Tony wished he were a little more like Ramiro. He needed to be less timid and do more mindless and crazy things.

Ramiro approached Tony and threw a left hook in the direction of Tony's ribs, stopping his punch before making contact. Ramiro was a skilled boxer and threw his irritating left hook as a way of greeting.

"Torrecita, what?" Ramiro said, grinning. "Still a virgin?"

Tony was shorter than Ramiro, but he did not like it when Ramiro called him Torrecita, a diminutive for de la Torre.

"I'm not too eager to get crabs, Ramiro. Have you gotten crabs lately?"

"I bet you didn't even try to talk to the girls at the pool."

"No. I'm waiting for Casanova to show me how it's done."

"I'm your man, Torrecita. Girls cannot resist me."

Unfortunately, there was some truth to that statement. Cristina de la Torre, another cousin, told Tony that girls considered

Ramiro very good looking. Ramiro was especially pleased with his hair—thick, straight, black, always perfectly combed. He could never pass a mirror without stopping to admire his appearance and check his hair, adjusting it just slightly.

Tony did not feel so good about his own hair; it was too curly and too blond, and the sun and salt water bleached it nearly white every summer. He did not look Cuban. On one occasion, he went to a Negro neighborhood in Old Havana to have his hair straightened so he could comb it straight back, like Ramiro. He was the only white boy in the barbershop, and he felt out of place and embarrassed. Afterward, he felt very attractive for a week, but then his hair curled up again.

They got their snorkeling equipment from the locker room and swam out from the beach. The water was getting murkier every year, probably because there were too many motorboats. They snorkeled for a while and then swam back to the Club and climbed up on the floating wooden platform at the tip of the Yacht Club's pier. They sat there for a while, dangling their finned feet over the water, making little splashes.

They were watching the bathers at La Concha, the public beach next to the Yacht Club. The same American architect who had designed the Capitol designed La Concha's Moorish style buildings and pavilions. It was considered the best public beach in Havana. It featured a concrete diving platform with several diving boards, fifty yards from the shore. In the middle of the platform stood a giant twenty-foot Cerveza Hatuey bottle—an ad for the beer company that donated the platform. The boys in Ramiro's group considered climbing the bottle and diving from the cap another test of manhood.

La Concha, in Tony's mind, was potentially a very sexy beach. This was the beach where young maids went and where the working girls he watched on his strolls on 23rd Street went whenever they had a Saturday off. Many female bathers at La Concha were those new modern Cuban women that Gonzalo talked about—all sex fiends.

Tony had also noticed that many prostitutes worked at La Concha. They were easy to spot. They picked up men at the beach and walked across the street, in their bathing suits, to a *posada*—a one-hour motel. The rooms went for one dollar, while the prostitutes charged two dollars.

"Let's swim over to La Concha and talk to the prostitutes," Ramiro said.

"Talk about what?"

"We can pretend we want to take them to a *posada*. Maybe they will let us feel them up."

"I doubt it, Ramiro. They are not stupid."

"Don't be silly, Torrecita. It's what they do—they talk to men and try to make a sale. Don't be such a chicken. Come on, follow me."

He put on his mask and splashed over the side.

"Let's go," he said, treading water.

If he didn't go, Tony thought, Ramiro would spend the rest of the day calling him a chicken. If he went with him, there was going to be trouble. Ramiro was now swimming on his back. *"No seas ratón!"* he yelled. Don't be a mouse.

Tony felt he did not have a choice. He put on his mask, jumped in and followed him.

At first, they looked at women underwater. As long as they kept a reasonable distance, nobody seemed to notice or mind. Very quickly, Tony started enjoying the snorkeling expedition. He particularly liked to watch lovers—there was always some fondling going on underwater. In deeper water, he watched four young women treading water, their thigh muscles flexing rhythmically, an erotic water ballet. It was hypnotic.

Tony was hoping that Ramiro had forgotten his original plan. Watching girls underwater was interesting and fun. But Ramiro had been scanning the beach for candidates all the while, and he spotted two girls standing in waist-deep water. One of them was striking, with bleached blond hair, like Marilyn Monroe. Marilyn was very popular in Havana. She had the kind of voluptuous body Cuban men favored and was often a feature in Havana magazines. The other girl was even more attractive, with long straight dark hair that fell down to her waist. They might have been around twenty years old, and the way they smiled at men hinted they could be prostitutes.

Ramiro suggested they stare at this pair and smile. Tony felt foolish, but he went along. It was awkward. It was hard for him to fake a smile. Ramiro knew what he was doing because the two women noticed them and started smiling back. The dark-haired woman raised an arm out of the water and beckoned them to join them.

"I told you," Ramiro said, grinning. He led the way as they waded toward them. Tony was nervous, but also curious. This was going to be embarrassing, but he could count on Ramiro to do most of the talking. Tony surprised himself by offering his hand to the dark-haired woman.

"Hello. My name is Tony."

"You are very polite," she said, shaking his hand.

Her green eyes stunned him. They were unusual and strange and beautiful. One of his favorite boleros, *Aquellos Ojos Verdes*, was about a girl with green eyes.

She was holding on to his hand, in no rush to let go. "My name is Sonia, handsome."

Tony liked being called handsome.

"So tell me," she said. "Are you boys spending a day at the beach with your mothers?" Sonia let go of his hand.

"No," Ramiro broke in.

"I was wondering why you boys were smiling at us," Sonia said.

"I was thinking that maybe we could do some business," Ramiro said, trying to sound experienced.

Damn, Tony thought. What if they were not prostitutes? For all he knew, they could have been young nuns just being friendly, spending a day at the beach, trying to convert some bathers. He thought that Ramiro should have slowed down and started with a more normal conversation.

"Wonderful!" Sonia said. She turned to her friend. "Magali, aren't these boys cute?"

"Tell me," she said, turning back to them. "You boys know how to masturbate already?"

They might be prostitutes after all, Tony thought.

"We were thinking," Ramiro said. "We could go to a *posada* with you, if you don't charge too much."

"Oh my, this one is very advanced for his age," Sonia said. "A child lover-boy looking for a bargain. You can have him, Magali. I prefer shy little Blondie. Tell me, Blondie, what's a Cuban boy like you doing with blond hair and blue eyes?"

Tony had been asked this question before. There was an answer, which he offered. His de la Torre grandfather had blue eyes and had married an O'Kindelan from Santiago, a Cuban family of Irish descent.

Sonia moved closer and smiled seductively. "Cuban and Irish!" She laughed, adding, "This one could be very good in bed. I also bet you boys don't have a cent on you."

"We don't have it on us," Ramiro said. "But we can get it from our club next door."

"Oh good," Sonia said. "Two little rich boys from the Havana Yacht Club! Let me guess. You want to touch my tits before you bring the money."

"Yes, if you don't mind," Ramiro said, grinning foolishly.

Sonia ignored Ramiro. She was focused on Tony.

"I bet that Blondie doesn't have any pubic hair yet," she said.

Tony was speechless. It was surprising to hear a woman talk this way. It was doubly surprising to hear a woman talk about *his* pubic hair.

Sonia moved closer. "Blondie," she said. "I'm going to have to check. Magali and I have moral standards. We don't do it with kids without pubic hair."

Before Tony could react, she circled him from behind, stuck her right hand inside his bathing suit and held on to his private parts.

Tony experienced some type of paralysis.

"Blondie," she said, pressed on to him from behind. "You barely pass the pubic hair test."

Sonia let her verdict sink in, then whispered in Tony's ear: "Blondie, come back with five dollars next Saturday. I promise you. You won't regret it."

Her hand lingered there for a few more seconds. "Don't forget," she whispered again. "Saturday. Five dollars." She pulled out her hand.

"Come, Magali," she said. "We'll let the boys get back to their mothers."

They waded off toward the sand, talking and laughing. Tony was still shocked from Sonia's surprising move. He stared at her while she emerged from the water and noticed that she had an excellent figure. He was thinking she had not been too serious about her whispered promise, but Sonia must have read his mind. She turned around and yelled: "Don't forget, Blondie!"

He did not forget. How could he forget? He had just acquired some excellent material for a fresh round of bad thoughts.

All week long he thought about Sonia, imagining a Saturday afternoon spent in a little room at the *posada*. In his fantasy, Sonia confessed to him: "You know, Blondie, thirteen-year-old blond, blue-eyed boys are my weakness. My obsession." Then she held his hand and led him to the bed, a small cot with clean white sheets. She took her time with him, introducing him to sexual pleasure. All the while, he was lost in her green eyes.

He also worried about other possible scenarios: Sonia laughed when she saw his small penis; he didn't know what to do in bed; Sonia had criminal friends hidden in the motel, waiting to kidnap him and ask his parents for ransom; she gave him crabs. Still, these thoughts did not last long. He could not explain why, but he trusted Sonia. Maybe she did feel especially attracted to young, blue-eyed Cuban boys. Maybe she meant it when she said he was handsome. She had focused on him, and not on Ramiro, who everyone agreed was handsome. He even liked how she called him Blondie.

His encounter with Sonia was making him reconsider his self-image. After a lifetime of being timid—a mouse, as Ramiro had called him, Sonia was presenting him with the opportunity to do something dramatic: to try on a new, more exciting and more risk-taking personality. He needed to be more of a doer, as Gonzalo had advised. If he lost his virginity, he would get Gonzalo and Ramiro off his back. And he would be doing it with Sonia, who had gorgeous green eyes and thought he was handsome. He seemed to trust her, and she seemed to like him.

It was a perfect match.

He was so focused on Sonia the whole week that it was hard for him to pay attention to his family at the dinner table, or to the Jesuits at school, or to Gonzalo and his theories about women. When Saturday came around, he was determined to act. At the club, he did not look for Ramiro. He thought that this was something that he wanted to do on his own. He changed into his bathing suit, walked to the tip of the Yacht Club's pier, dove into the warm water with five American dollars tucked in his bathing suit pocket and swam over to la Concha.

Sonia was nowhere to be found.

He waited for her until lunch when he went back to the Yacht Club. He ate lunch quickly and returned to La Concha. He walked up and down the beachfront all afternoon, searching for her.

At five-thirty he noticed that Gonzalo was at the tip of the Yacht Club's pier, looking for him. When Gonzalo spotted Tony at La Concha, sitting dejectedly by the water's edge, he yelled at him to hurry back. Gonzalo was upset because he had to be back at the house to drive Cocó to a dinner.

Tony knew then that his adventure with Sonia was not going to happen. It had been his first attempt to do something about his sexual impulses, something courageous on his own initiative, but Sonia had let him down. She completely forgot about him and what she had promised the previous week.

He felt terrible about being stood up, but he would tell no one. Especially not Ramiro. He could imagine Ramiro, gleefully reminding him for the rest of his life how he was the first man in the history of Havana to be stood up by a prostitute.

5

THE FOLLOWING SATURDAY TONY decided to skip snorkeling and swim some laps in the pool instead. There were a few girls there from his age group—Carmen Maciá, Lola Sampedro, and the Delgado sisters. The Delgado sisters were silly, and Lola Sampedro was as skinny as a rail, but he could not find one shortcoming with Carmen Macía. If he had any courage in him, he would go up to her and start a conversation.

The four girls were lying face down on large towels, tanning their backs. He had known them since he was three or four, when he started going to their birthday parties. Some of those parties were elaborate affairs where all the children wore the same costumes. He remembered one party during which he dressed as a member of a military band and another one where everyone was dressed as an angel. He remembered hating the outfits, especially

the angel one, which had unbearably ridiculous wings. But he had
to attend those parties because his parents and the girls' parents
grew up together; went to the same schools, the same clubs, sum-
mered on the same beach and were listed in the same hardcover
telephone book known as the Social Guide.

The Social Guide included not only the families that belonged
to the Havana Yacht Club, but also members of the other upper
class clubs, like the Vedado Tennis Club, the Biltmore Yacht Club,
and the Havana Country Club. There must have been over a thousand families listed in the Social Guide, and most of them knew
each other.

Soon, most likely this summer, the girls' birthdays would be
occasions for dance parties. Those dance parties would start the
process of pairing-off. Tony was not looking forward to those parties. He was a terrible dancer. He couldn't imagine why anyone
would want to pair off with him and, someday, marry him.

Still, the odds were good that he would marry one of the girls
at those parties or one of the girls sunbathing by the pool at the
Havana Yacht Club. Upper class Havana families did not marry
outside the Social Guide.

At the moment, though, it was a struggle for Tony to talk to
his prospective brides. He had not found it easy talking to them
when he was dressed as an angel, and he was having more problems now, as an adolescent, with his mind overflowing with perverted thoughts. All the girls in his group had shown up for the
new beach season at the Yacht Club with brand new, almost full-
grown breasts. It made the ordeal of talking to them that much
more challenging.

It was also hard to figure out what interests the girls shared
with him. They were not interested in fishing or baseball, and he
doubted they were interested in his current obsessions—mastur-

bating and having sexual fantasies. The nuns who taught them made it very clear that anything dealing with sex was a major sin and something to avoid until they were married. A new movie release was one possible topic of conversation. Funny stories circulating about mutual friends were another. New jokes were also good conversation material, but that topic was unavailable to Tony because he could never remember the punch lines.

Being funny was important. Cubans unanimously agreed that being funny and making people laugh were the highest virtues. The opposite of being funny, *ser un pesado*, was the worst sin. Nothing—not money, intelligence or good looks—could redeem a bore.

Still, Tony suspected that what the girls from good families mostly wanted from a future mate was the means to maintain their lifestyle. They all wanted enormous houses with seven or eight servants, similar to their parents' houses. Before he considered those girls as possible mates, and before they considered him, he had to come up with a career that paid for the eight servants and a house to put them in. He had to come up with a very profitable career because he was not going to inherit anything from his father.

His father had never had much success at making money. Victor de la Torre lived in his father-in-law's house, didn't have any expenses, didn't work, and mostly played bridge and golf—two activities he excelled at. All Tony was going to inherit was a good family name, and even that was probably being devalued by the current generation of de la Torres.

Tony walked up to the pool's diving board and dove in. He was an excellent diver, and maybe the girls would notice that. He was good at all water sports: fishing, skin-diving, water skiing, swimming, diving and holding his breath under water. Not many career prospects in any of those activities, though.

He swam about ten laps, came out and sat upright on a deck chair. He looked toward the four girls and noticed they had not changed positions. Ten very fast laps had gone unnoticed. He needed to do more. He considered boldly walking up to them and starting a conversation with Carmen. He could start the conversation by asking her if she had seen his cousin Tina lately. Carmen and Tina were best friends.

He had known Carmen for years; she had been a guest at the angels party—he could recognize her in the photograph of that party in his mother's album—but he had never talked to her until last summer.

Last summer, he visited his cousin Tina's cattle ranch in Cama-guey Province near a little town called Ciego de Avila. Tina, Carmen and Luis, Tina's younger brother, were there, and the four of them did everything together. Tía Nina, Tina's mom, called them the four musketeers. His uncle had a stable full of horses, and they rode every day. His impression of Carmen then was that she was funny, pretty and a bit of a tomboy. She rode as well as he did, and when they played together at a pick-up baseball game, she smacked the baseball hard and ran fast to first base.

This summer, Carmen looked more like a woman. What a difference one year had made. She had terrific breasts, her waist had narrowed and her hips had some heft to them. He overheard a boy in the locker room say that Carmen Macía *estaba buenísima*. Tony couldn't agree more.

Instead of walking toward the four girls to start a conversation, Tony leaned back on the deck chair and closed his eyes. Could he imagine making love to Carmen Maciá? It could happen, many years from now, after he graduated from college, and after they married. Their first night together would be a night to remember. Carmen would bring a long history of frustrated sexual desires, years of going out with chaperones and living by the rules of Cuban culture, which did not permit her to kiss a man or be touched by one; and suddenly there she would be, lying naked under linen sheets next to the man she had just married, and anything they did would be acceptable. Even the church would applaud, as long as the ultimate goal was to produce many Catholic babies.

He opened his eyes and looked at the girls again. They had turned. They were tanning themselves on a timer. He thought again about the vacation he spent with Carmen and his two cousins in Ciego.

The four of them got up early every morning, saddled the horses and explored every corner of the ranch. It was a large ranch. It had forests, prairies, a river and even a small mountain. They rode fast, raced often and afterward went for a swim in the river. They particularly enjoyed swinging into the river, Tarzan-like, on the rope they had attached to a tree branch high up on a bank.

After lunch, they played Ping-Pong on the porch and then napped. Later in the day, they played tennis at the local country club. At night, they went to the movies or played poker for pennies. During all these activities, Tony and Carmen talked, joked, flirted and competed. Tony was the oldest and therefore the one everyone wanted to beat at horse races, Ping-Pong and tennis.

He especially remembered one night. It was a particularly hot night, and it was going to be impossible to sleep. They decided to walk to the river and go swimming. They went in and floated in the warm water. Afterward, they stretched out on towels on a sandy area at the river's edge. They laid there, touching elbows, staring at the stars, listening to the cacophony of crickets, owls and frogs. Carmen was next to him, and Tony was aware how their thighs were touching. Above them, they could see a textbook Milky Way and, every now and then, a shooting star. They started counting the shooting stars, which started a discussion about where the shooting stars came from. That got them talking about the universe and the immensity of it all, and the meaning, or the meaningless, of life. All the while, Tony was thinking about the meaning of Carmen not moving her thigh away.

That had to mean something.

And here was Carmen again. He wanted to go up to her and say hello.

Instead, Tony swam some more laps. He swam ten more laps, as fast as he could. When he finished the last lap, he glanced at the girls again. They were lying face down. They had ignored him again! He would say hello to Carmen some other day.

He came out of the pool and started walking toward the locker room. It bothered him that he did not talk to Carmen. He wished he were more sociable, or outgoing or more self-confident.

6

TONY SHOWERED, DRESSED AND
was tying his shoelaces when a boy he knew by sight, Emilio Eloy,
entered the room and started undressing in a nearby locker. Tony
had heard stories about him; mostly that he was a bit crazy and an
agitador, someone who enjoyed provoking fights. In fact, he was
one of the few boys even Ramiro was afraid of, but Emilio did not
strike Tony as a bully.

Emilio was not much bigger than Tony, but looked stronger
and older, although Tony suspected they were the same age. One
immediately noticed Emilio's black hair, combed straight back like
Rudolph Valentino. Emilio grinned constantly, as if everything
that happened around him was amusing.

Tony foresaw trouble when he casually looked toward Emilio
and saw that he was staring at him. Tony quickly averted his glance,
but it was no use. Emilio started singing:

I know a cute little blond boy
She's so cute
And she sneaks into the boys' locker room to tie her
    shoes.

This song obviously referred to Tony, but he pretended he was not listening. Emilio continued singing, this time louder:

This little blond girl
She has a very nice ass
And she doesn't hear too well!

Emilio bellowed the last line. Tony was thinking that Emilio's reputation, as a troublemaker, was apparently true.

Tony knew he had to do something. There were a few boys around, watching, but Tony was not planning to say anything that could lead to a fight. During his last fight, in the sixth grade, he was knocked-out cold by the school bully. From then on, his strategy was to talk his way out of fights without doing too much damage to his dignity.

A little ego damage was preferable to some brain damage.

One simple strategy to avoid a fight was to pretend that he did not hear whomever called him a *maricón*, a *hijo de puta*, a little blond girl, or whatever other insult was sent at him, so he could just walk away.

In this situation, however, it was going to be difficult to pretend that he had not heard Emilio.

"You want to fight?" Tony said to Emilio, surprising everybody, including himself.

"Anytime, little blond girl!" Emilio said, seemingly delighted. He moved uncomfortably close to Tony.

"Why? I don't even know you," Tony replied, moving away.

"Because I called you a girl with a nice ass, that's why."

What an idiot, Tony thought, even though he heard a few chuckles from the other boys.

"If you think I'm a girl, you need glasses," Tony said, trying to appear calm.

"Okay. You are not a girl. You are a *maricón!*" Emilio bellowed again, and then he laughed, pleased with his wit.

At least he laughed, Tony thought. "You can think whatever you want. It doesn't bother me." He figured that was an adequate exit line, and he delivered it calmly. He could feel his heart pounding as he walked around Emilio and left the locker room.

THE following weekend Tony was not too eager to go to the Yacht Club, but on Sunday his entire family went to the club for lunch, and he had to go, too. After lunch his grandfather excused himself and headed for a game room on the second floor to play dominoes. His father made a beeline to the bar to drink scotch and play *cubilete*, a dice game. His mother and grandmother went to the ladies game room to play canasta. The children were left on their own.

Tony was not planning to go swimming and risk running into Emilio in the locker room again. Then, like in a movie with a fast moving plot, Emilio came into the dining room. He walked straight to Tony's table. Was he going to provoke him again in front of his family? How crazy was he?

"You are Tony de la Torre, right?" Emilio said, smiling. "My father told me you're going to be one of my classmates at Choate this September."

Tony knew that other Cuban boys were going to start with him at Choate, the prep school in Connecticut where his father and uncles had gone, but he never expected Emilio would be one of them. He thought one had to be smart to get accepted to Choate.

"I was kidding you in the locker room the other day," Emilio was now saying. "Do you want to be friends?"

"Yes," Tony said, thinking he'd rather be Emilio's friend than his punching bag.

"Would you like to come to my house for lunch next Saturday?"

"Yes," Tony said.

IT was a thirty-minute drive from Tony's house in the Vedado section to Emilio's house in the Country Club section. The Country Club section offered wealthy Cubans something that the Vedado section did not have: space. The houses there had large grounds and beautiful gardens.

Tony was curious about Emilio's family. Emilio's father was a colorful and well-known businessman—the president and founder of a large insurance company. His company's jingles ran constantly on the radio: *"Para seguros de hoy, Seguros Eloy."* For today's insurance, Insurance Eloy.

Gonzalo drove past the large Corpus Christi church, which stood at the bottom of the hilly Country Club section. The Eloys lived a few blocks beyond the church, around the corner from the Fanjul house, where his parents often went to dinner parties. Gonzalo turned into the Eloy driveway, past elaborate iron gates, into a cobblestone courtyard where Emilio and the Eloys' chauffeur were peering under the hood of a white Mercedes touring car. Behind them stood a large French-Chateau style mansion.

Gonzalo knew Roberto, the Eloys' chauffeur, and they exchanged greetings. All chauffeurs in Havana knew each other; they waited together for their employers outside the same clubs and the same parties. Tony got out of the car and watched as Gonzalo stepped on the gas and screeched out of the driveway. Tony smiled. He guessed Gonzalo was headed to a nearby apartment to perform his moral duty.

"Tony," Emilio said, amused as he watched Gonzalo's dramatic departure. "I want you to meet Roberto, our chauffeur. He's a very slow driver compared to your chauffeur."

Roberto laughed and shook hands with Tony. Emilio suggested they go to his room while they waited for lunch. "I want to show you something," he said. They went in through a back door, into a large kitchen area, past a busy group of servants, into a vestibule area, then up a curving marble staircase.

"You know," Emilio said, as they were walking up the stairs. "Roberto is the only chauffeur in Havana who can claim to have played roulette in Monaco. Last summer he drove us all over Europe after we picked up the Mercedes in Germany."

Tony was quickly getting the message. Emilio's father was exceptionally rich, richer than Tony's grandfather Cocó, not to mention richer than his father. Still, Tony was not overly impressed. Just the fact that Emilio talked about a European trip to pick up a Mercedes meant that he felt the need to brag about it; their money was undoubtedly new money. He had picked up from family conversations that if one had money and one was well-bred, it was not necessary, nor polite, to talk about it. He expected Emilio's parents to have terrible taste and horrible manners. Tony's grandmother often said that manners and taste were the first line of defense of old money against new money.

However, even if Mr. Eloy had horrible manners, it would not bother Tony. He admired people like Mr. Eloy, who started a successful business from scratch, as opposed to many of his father's friends who simply inherited land or businesses. If Tony ever hoped to have money, he would have to do it the hard way, from scratch, like what Mr. Eloy had done.

Emilio's room was twice as large as Tony's room. In the center, on a wooden platform, was an immense canopied mahogany double bed with three wooden steps leading up to it. Tony's first thought was that Emilio would announce that his bed had once belonged to some French king, bought at auction. His intuition was not far off. He later learned that Emilio's father was an admirer of Napoleon and had a collection of letters signed by him. He also owned one of Napoleon's urinals. Julio Lobo, the richest man in Cuba, also owned a Napoleon urinal in addition to other Napoleon artifacts. Emilio's dad and Julio Lobo apparently had a Napoleon urinal competition.

The first thing that Emilio showed Tony was an entire dresser filled only with his polo shirts. He said he bought them at Abercrombie and Fitch in New York, and he had one in every color. On top of this dresser, and on the other cabinets, there were a large number of framed photographs. Many of the pictures were of Emilio and his teammates mounted on polo ponies, receiving a trophy from someone on foot, all smiling for the camera.

Emilio noticed Tony looking at the pictures.

"I've been playing competitive polo since I was eight. I've broken two bones already. I've played with Porfirio Rubirosa."

"Who is that?"

"Tony, what are you, a caveman!"

"Why?"

"You've never heard of Porfirio Rubirosa?"

"No."

"He's a famous international playboy from the Dominican Republic. He married two of the world's wealthiest women."

Emilio was starting to irritate Tony. He was a showoff.

Still, Tony was intrigued. He didn't know anyone else who

played polo with playboys.

"Have you necked yet?" Emilio asked.

"No."

"I have. I also belong to the Biltmore Yacht Club. I became a member just to meet American girls. I went to an American party near the Biltmore last week, and I necked with two different girls during the party."

What a showoff, Tony thought, even though he was impressed because what Emilio said could have been true. American girls were very popular among Cuban boys. Everyone knew that they danced close, they drank, they kissed, they necked, and they didn't go out with chaperones. He would have loved to meet an American girl. The older boys he knew at the Yacht Club habitually combed the hotels and casinos at night trying to meet American girls on vacation. The American colony living in Havana was tougher to crack; they stuck to their own.

"Have you gone to a brothel?" Emilio asked, moving on to the next topic.

"No. Have you?" Tony expected him to say yes.

"No, but I'm going to go soon. Would you like to go with me?"

"I don't know," Tony said, unprepared for that question.

"My father and I have talked about it," Emilio said. "He told me that whenever I'm ready, I could go to a brothel. He only wants to make sure I go to a clean place."

"You talk about going to a brothel with your father?"

"Sure. We talk about everything."

Tony thought how he rarely talked to his father.

"I want to go to the Mambo Club," Emilio said. "Do you know of it?"

"Sure," Tony said.

"The Mambo Club guarantees that they won't get crabs or

gonorrhea," Emilio said.

"I have heard that," Tony said.

There was a pause in the conversation, and Tony dwelled on the warranty offered by the Mambo. If it were true, that would make the Mambo more appealing. The thought of a colony of crabs crawling around in his pubic hair and sucking his blood was a horrible thought. The thought of even scarier diseases, like syphilis, was worse.

There was a de la Torre family story that Ramiro's mother had told him, the story of his great aunt Margarita who was reputed to be one of the most beautiful women in Havana at the turn of the century. Every afternoon, at five, she went out for a carriage ride around the Prado Boulevard, and every day at that time the sidewalks of the Prado filled with men who lined up to catch a glimpse of her. As she passed, the men tipped their hats, hoping to catch her attention. She was beautiful, she was very wealthy, and she was single.

When the time came for Margarita to marry, she fell in love with the man whom everyone knew was a disaster. He was a known womanizer who frequented the brothels, and he didn't work because he lived on a small inheritance. But he was very handsome, he made Margarita laugh and she fell for him. Margarita's father, a prominent lawyer, prohibited the marriage, and Margarita refused to marry any of the approved prospects. Margarita was in her thirties when her father died, and she immediately married the womanizer, who by then had syphilis. Margarita also contracted syphilis, and both died horrible deaths.

A hand bell rang downstairs.

"That's lunch," Emilio said. "I forgot! I wanted to show you something." He led Tony out of his room. The hallway outside was lined with windows, facing the cobblestone courtyard. Emilio went over to one of the windows and swung it open.

"Come here, watch this." He took off his watch, grinned at Tony, and then threw the watch out the window.

"Damn, why did you do that?"

"It's a Rolex, 100% shock resistant. I got it for my birthday. Let me show you."

They went down the stairs and out the front door. Emilio picked up the watch and looked at it.

"See, it's still working," he said, smiling.

EMILIO'S parents were older than Tony's parents, around fifty, but they looked fit, and well groomed. Mrs. Eloy seemed to have a very agreeable personality. She smiled constantly, like Emilio. Emilio kissed her on both cheeks, European style.

Emilio's father was short—just over five feet. It explained his interest in Napoleon, but he had a great posture, a way of standing very erect, which more than made up for his lack of stature. He was wearing an ascot and a white linen jacket, which matched his hair, white, thick, and combed straight back. He could have played the role of a successful American financier in a Hollywood movie.

"Tony, it's a pleasure to meet you," he said, firmly shaking Tony's hand. "I'm delighted you're going to be one of my son's companions at Choate. I know your de la Torre family, a delightful family!"

Tony's family was amusing, no doubt, but he wished they were less amusing and harder working, like Mr. Eloy.

"So both of you are off to Choate in September," he said, still holding on firmly to Tony's hand. "I know you will be a very good example for my son Emilio. I worry about him. I don't know if he has told you, but Emilio is not one of the world's best students. We are all going to have to work hard on his study habits."

"I'm probably one of the world's worst students!" Emilio broke in, laughing.

Emilio's father chuckled at his son's outburst. That chuckle, Tony thought, said a lot about Mr. Eloy. He not only accepted Emilio's shortcomings, but he also found them endearing and amusing. Mr. Eloy was easy to like.

Mr. Eloy led the way to a covered outdoor terrace where a lunch table was set. They sat down, and servants started bringing in trays with French-looking food. Tony had no idea what was being served. At his house they ate Cuban food; black beans and rice, fried plantains, roast pork, yucca.

"I was never a good student myself," Emilio's father said. "And I never went to college. I wish I had. But I'm still a student—a student of life. One of my passions is reading about the lives of great men. I'm a big admirer of Bernard Baruch, Winston Churchill and Franklin Roosevelt. I never went to college, but I know everything there is to know about these great men. I can tell you boys, there's only one lesson to be learned from them."

Mr. Eloy paused there, to emphasize what he was about to say. He looked at Emilio, then at Tony. Tony noticed that Emilio was busy gulping down his food. Emilio had probably heard this lesson before. Tony had not, and he was paying attention.

"You can accomplish anything you want if—and if is the crucial word—if you want it, if you put your mind to it and if you are willing to work for it. Those are the three ifs, boys. And when you think you may have failed, when you question yourself, when everything looks hopeless, there is only one way to proceed—you persevere, you push harder, you lean forward, you never quit."

Tony had never heard adults carry on in this way, and he was interested. These were lessons about life. They didn't teach those lessons at his school or at his house. Tony wanted to know why some people were successful businessmen, like Mr. Eloy, and why others were not successful, like his father. Success didn't depend on intelligence because he could tell his father was very intelligent. It was something else, and whatever it was, Mr. Eloy knew about it, and he seemed willing to share his insights.

Tony's father and his de la Torre uncles didn't seem too interested in the concept of success. They mostly talked about golf, bridge hands or told funny stories about their friends. They were interested in enjoying life and laughing as often as possible. But there was something to be said for that because everyone in Havana knew and liked the de la Torre brothers.

"Darling," Mrs. Eloy said, speaking for the first time. "I'm sure the boys don't want to hear about Bernard Baruch."

"Adela, there's nothing wrong with Bernard Baruch. He was a very wise man. I've learned many things from Bernard Baruch, and I've attempted to pass on those teachings to my son Emilio. But you are absolutely right, dear. One of the reasons I love your mother, Emilio, is that she is always right. Look at these boys eat, Adela! I'd like to do the same thing myself, but at my age I have to take care of myself."

"Come on dad, you're in great shape." Emilio turned to Tony. "My dad still plays polo. He's rated at four goals."

AFTER lunch, Emilio invited Tony to the movies. Roberto drove them to La Lisa Theater, in the Torrecilla section of Havana. The Torrecilla section was not a good neighborhood. In fact, it was downright seedy. Tony had never gone to La Lisa Theater, but he had heard about it from the older boys at the Yacht Club. They only played pornographic movies at La Lisa.

The movie playing that Saturday had a simple plot. It was an

Italian movie, with no subtitles, but this shortcoming did not seem to bother the audience. The main character appeared to be an art director for an advertising agency, whose current assignment was to find the model for an undergarment ad.

This low budget movie had one set, the art director's studio. A succession of eager, innocent and luscious candidates arrived to apply for the job. After a few pleasantries, the art director got down to business. He must have said something like: "Miss, now you can take off your clothes." The young women were shocked. They protested, but they wanted the job. Then each candidate took off everything except the panties, slowly, very slowly, one garment at a time. The camera caressed every move while the enthusiastic all-male audience at La Lisa participated with loud hoots, whistles and catcalls, the cacophony always reaching a crescendo with the removal of the last item: the bra.

When the movie ended, Tony was in a daze. He had just seen his first pornographic movie. It had been interesting. They were walking toward the Mercedes, adjusting their eyes to the bright Havana sunlight.

"Let's go to the lingerie department at El Encanto," Emilio said.

"What for?" Tony replied.

"The movie has given me an idea. You'll see," Emilio said, smiling.

El Encanto, Havana's oldest and most expensive department store, was Tony's mother's favorite store. On Saturdays, shoppers jammed the store. Tony still could not imagine what they were going to do there. Emilio led him to the second floor, the women's area, and made his way to a counter where two young female attendants sold brassieres.

"Miss," he called to one of the attendants. "Could you help

me, please?"

A young woman moved over. She was around twenty, snappily dressed, very pleased with her appearance.

"I'm interested in buying a bra for my girlfriend," Emilio said, in a matter-of-fact manner. "It's her birthday. I want a black one, maybe with lace."

The young woman hesitated. She was not used to selling bras to thirteen-year-old boys.

"I can show you some samples. Do you know her size?"

"I don't remember the number, but can you turn to your side?"

Tony was starting to understand Emilio's little game. He had some nerve.

"What for?" she said with a blank expression.

"I think she's about your size, and if I could get a better look at you in profile, I think I could tell better."

She laughed. "You must be joking," she said.

"I'm not joking," Emilio said. "Miss, I'm trying to buy a bra." He looked appropriately hurt. Emilio was quite an actor.

She looked at Emilio, considered the situation and then forced a smile. "I'll bring you a few choices. 34B."

They waited for the bras to arrive. The other woman at the counter had been listening to the conversation. By the way she was looking at them, Tony could almost hear her thinking: What gall, the little clown!

The attendant returned with two boxes.

"Here are two bras, black with lace, which I'm sure your girl-friend will like." She was businesslike, doing her job, but Tony could tell that if it were up to her, she would have them thrown out of the store.

Emilio opened one of the boxes, took out the bra and placed it on the counter. Slowly and meticulously, like a magician about to perform a trick, he cupped his left hand, the tips of all five fingers touching. Then over this construction, he carefully placed one of the cups of the bra. He closed his eyes. With his other hand, he fondled the cup.

Tony could barely keep a straight face.

Emilio opened his eyes. "This one doesn't feel right," he said. "I think it's too small. Miss, could you bring me the larger size?"

Tony had to admire Emilio. He was obnoxious, but he had a lot of nerve. The world of adults, and its rules, did not intimidate him. Tony had never met a boy quite like him.

The woman at the counter, though, did not think Emilio's little performance was amusing. She was not impressed by his boldness. A dark cloud was forming in her eyes.

"It's going to cost you ten pesos," she said curtly.

Emilio was not through yet. Like an actor, aware of a great performance, he pulled out his wallet, slowly took out two five-peso bills and put the money on the counter.

"Miss, I'll buy the bra, but I'm still uncertain about the size. If you don't mind, can I feel your breasts for a second? Then I'd know for sure if they are the same size."

Damn, Tony thought, this guy is crazy.

"I'm calling the guard!" she said and quickly walked away.

They were out of there fast.

7

SUNDAY'S LUNCH AT COCÓ'S WAS usually the best meal of the week, and everyone in his family had been anticipating this one because Rolando had prepared stuffed lobsters. Tony decided to pay close attention to the table conversation, intent on comparing his family's conversation with the conversation at the Eloys' table the previous day. The conversation at the Eloys had impressed him, especially the part about what it took to succeed in life.

His family was seated at their usual places. Cocó sat at the head of the long mahogany table, and Nana, Tony's grandmother, sat at the other end. Cocó's two daughters, Tony's mother, Lydia, and his aunt Julia, flanked him. Tony's dad and his uncle Julio sat next to their spouses. The two oldest grandchildren, Tony and his sister Sofi, sat facing each other next to Nana. Tony's three younger siblings, Lydia, who was nine, Cristina, eight and Victor Jr., five, ate at the little table set in the pantry with his aunt's young son, Julito. The pantry was a large room between the dining room and the kitchen. Tony's younger siblings and Julito would not move up to the big table until they were at least eleven or twelve.

Lunch started with Gazpacho soup, which Rolando made to perfection. Cocó was pleased and quickly told the butler to tell Rolando that the soup was superb. Cocó's message to the kitchen gave Tony a curious feeling of déjà-vu. His father had recently told a story during a previous Sunday lunch that had included a similar message to the kitchen. That story was about his father's first cook at La Estrella, Don Antonio's sugar mill in Camaguey Province.

Victor's first order of business had been to set up a household for himself and his new bride in a small house next to the large family house at La Estrella. He had hired a few maids and, most importantly, the cook. The cook had come highly recommended, and he turned out to be much better than expected. A few weeks had passed when Tony's dad invited Don Antonio to dinner, mostly to show off his new cook. The first few plates were brought in, and Don Antonio quickly agreed that the cook was very good. He made it a point to tell the maid to tell the cook that the food was excellent. Don Antonio was so impressed that after dinner, he proposed going to the kitchen to meet and congratulate the cook; his name was Angelito, little angel, a name that belied his appearance: Angelito was an enormously fat man. Tony's dad sensed trouble and insisted that it was not necessary for his father to go to the kitchen to congratulate the cook. He would make sure the cook heard about his approval. But Don Antonio insisted. He went to the kitchen, told Angelito that the food was very good, went back to the dining table, and told Victor to fire the cook the next day.

"Fire him!" Victor was shocked. "Why? Didn't you just tell him that the food was excellent?"

"The food was very good, Victor," Don Antonio had replied. "But I don't trust fat men, especially in the kitchen."

Everyone laughed at the punch line, even though they laughed nervously because Cocó was substantially overweight. Tony laughed too. It was a funny story, although he felt sorry for the cook. It didn't seem fair. But he knew about his de la Torre grandfather's phobia about fat people.

Cocó certainly didn't have that problem. He liked to eat. That Sunday he had enjoyed Rolando's *gazpacho* soup so much that he asked for seconds. Tony noticed that he had gulped down the soup so fast that he had been careless and spilled some soup on his white starched linen shirt.

Nana had also noticed: "Cocó, please! Try to be more careful."

Nana's mission in life was to improve and civilize Cocó, hoping to make him more palatable to a Havana society that was overly conscious of breeding and manners.

"Nana," Cocó replied. "Could you let me enjoy my meal! So I spilled some soup on my shirt. So what?"

That ended the conversation. Cocó was usually civil, Tony thought, but he had a temper. As family patriarch and sole bill payer, he made it clear that he had the right to end any conversation not to his liking.

Tony noticed that his father did not look too pleased with Cocó's outburst. He probably was not too pleased with his table manners either. Soup was never spilled on shirts on his father's side of the family.

Tony knew that his dad and Cocó had a complicated relationship. They were polite to each other, but Cocó didn't approve of how his dad was often unemployed. Cocó was a hard working man, and he still put in long hours at his office. He disapproved of how his son-in-law spent most days at the Havana Country Club. Victor, in turn, was not too impressed with Cocó because, Tony guessed, he wasn't a sportsman, he wasn't that well educated and, as his dad often claimed, he didn't have a sense of humor—all the qualities the de la Torres admired and excelled at.

The de la Torres and the Campos also came from different backgrounds. The de la Torre family was a large, boisterous and old Cuban family with a long history of accomplishments and wealth. Cocó's family came from a small town in Matanzas Province. They were hard working and honorable people with a long history of modest means and modest accomplishments. Cocó had broken with that tradition. He had a mind for business, and each of his business ventures had been extremely profitable. Tony couldn't keep track of all the things that Cocó owned—around 10 apartment buildings in Havana, sugar lands around various sugar mills and two large cattle ranches. He deserved a lot of credit, but in Tony's mind, he much preferred the de la Torres. That side of the family was more fun.

Tony loved hearing his father tell stories about his childhood. The de la Torre family compound, built on the de la Torre family tradition of owning sugar mills, occupied almost a whole block in Amargura Street in Old Havana. His father grew up there with eight sets of aunts and uncles and 30 first cousins. In those days, if the patriarch had enough money, it was considered downright impolite for the sons or daughters to move out when they married, so families stayed together and family compounds grew to enormous sizes.

His dad had so many first cousins living with him on Amargura Street that every day after school the cousins went to a nearby park and fielded two baseball teams. The little table at the compound on Amargura Street was not so little; it regularly served up to twenty children and ten nannies in one sitting. Moving to the big table was a major rite of passage, where the criteria for graduation was not only age, but manners and conversation, as determined by Don Miguel, the patriarch of that household. Manners had to be impeccable, and the conversation had to be minimal. Children were to be seen, but not heard.

Tony's dad had a story about his first day at the big table: He was trying to crack the claw of a crab, using a silver claw-cracking tool he was not familiar with. He was squeezing hard on the claw when it slipped and shot off, skidding across the glass table until it bounced with a loud clink off Don Miguel's plate. Tony's dad was demoted back to the little table.

"Does anyone remember what happened the last time we had stuffed lobster?" Tony's dad was now saying, attempting to lighten the mood created by Cocó's outburst.

"I had it all figured out," Tony's dad continued. "Only Julia and Julio were left to be served in front of me, and there were six lobsters left. I calculated that Julio would take two, and Julia one, which would leave me three, and I was planning on taking all three. I was even thinking Julio might be overly polite and would only take one, which would leave me with the option of taking four. So what happened? Julio took two and Julia took four!"

Everyone laughed. Julia protested: "Victor, that's not true!"

Tony's father insisted it was true, and he and Julia argued about it. Then the women in the table started talking about a dinner party at the Countess Revilla-Comargo's Vedado mansion. She had a notoriously good French chef and the conversation revolved around the delicious desserts that the Countess had served.

The butler arrived with the second course, black beans and rice, followed by a tray of sweet plantains. Both plates were cooked perfectly. There was another round of praise for Rolando. Everyone in the family knew that Rolando was an excellent cook. They were fortunate to have him. They also knew that Cocó had a stormy relationship with Rolando. Whenever they got in a fight, tempers would escalate, Cocó would yell at Rolando, Rolando would quit and the whole family would cringe, including Cocó.

According to Gonzalo, the fights were always about money. Gonzalo claimed that Rolando had not one, but two mistresses, and even though he was the highest paid servant in Cocó's household at one hundred pesos a month, his complicated romantic life always left him short of cash at the end of the month.

Rolando tried to solve his finances by playing the numbers, which most Cubans played. He went over his dreams for signs—significant animals or strange objects—and he played them. If there was a rooster in his dream, and the rooster had done something unusual, then he played the rooster's number that day. For gambling purposes, everything under the sun was assigned a number. There was a bookie in every corner of the city.

However, Rolando never seemed to win. He would ask Cocó for advances. Cocó would respond by reminding Rolando that he had already forgiven him two or three advances that had never been repaid, that he had warned Rolando that there would be no more "advances," and that Rolando had to learn to live within his means like everyone else. Still, Rolando would insist that this time the advance was for a real emergency. Cocó would tell Rolando that that was what he had said the last time. Rolando would threaten to quit if he did not get the advance. At that point, the negotiations would break down: Cocó would start screaming, and Rolando would quit.

Rolando's absence never lasted long. Cocó was addicted to the way Rolando cooked the black beans, the *mojito* for the *yuca*, the red snapper in green sauce, the *ropa vieja* and the *caldo gallego*. He especially could not live without his *flanes* or nearly everything else that Rolando cooked. After a week of Cocó's daily complaints about how everything cooked by Ramón, Rolando's assistant, did not taste right, Nana would make a suggestion:

"Cocó, you know you only like Rolando's cooking. Why don't you offer to pay him the advance, this time for the last time, and send Gonzalo for him? He will gladly come back."

"Fine," Cocó would reply. "I'll do it this one more time, but I will insist that this is definitely the last time I will have him back."

Rolando would be summoned back, he would get his money and everything would run smoothly in the kitchen until the next advance request.

The plates were cleared, new plates were brought in, and the lobsters were served. Everyone gave more praise for the lobsters, especially for the stuffing. Tony's mother and his aunt Julia talked about the jewelry the countess wore, who had worn what and which dresses had been in bad taste.

José Ignacio was summoned for a second round of stuffed lobsters. Then Nana, in a somber tone, mentioned that Lydia de Cárdenas was in the Miramar hospital. The time had come for the conversation to deal with the dying and the sick. Wakes and hospital visits were a significant component of the Havana social scene. The sick never lacked visitors. Havana society was like one large family.

"I heard she has cancer," Nana continued. "We need to visit."

León mentioned he had also heard that Pedro de la Torriente was also at Miramar. It did not look promising for him either. The adults were silent for a while and worked on their lobsters. They probably thought about mortality and how lucky they were not to be sick. Then Cocó, who had been unusually quiet, made a surprise announcement.

"I got a call today from the King Ranch in Texas," he said, beaming. "I've been giving the call some thought. They are offering to buy my best ranch, Mariguá, for three million dollars!"

Everyone at the table was impressed. That was a lot of money.

"I thought about it, briefly, but I told them I would not sell Mariguá for 10 million!" Cocó let that sink in. "It's the finest cattle ranch in Cuba, and I have no intention of selling it."

"It is still wonderful, dear, that the Kleibergs are interested in Mariguá and are willing to offer that much for it," Nana said.

"If I were you, I would reconsider the offer." Tony's dad said.

"I'm curious, Victor. Why should I reconsider?"

Tony could tell that an argument was in the making.

"I would sell it right now because we are on the first year of a Batista dictatorship, and in a few years this economy will be in ruins. Batista and his ministers will steal every cent in the treasury; American investments in Cuba will dry up. The economy will go to hell and so will land prices. Five years from now, with three million dollars, you could buy three cattle ranches the size of Mariguá."

"Victor, I could not disagree with you more. Cuba has had dictators before, and none has lasted more than a few years. Batista will not last, like all the rest. My policy has always been to never get involved in politics, and it has served me well. Also, what would you know about selling something that has taken me a lifetime to build? You would not understand any of that. I have put Mariguá together, parcel by parcel, for the past twenty years. You tell me, who has a finer cattle ranch in this country? No one. I will never sell it."

"Cocó," Tony's dad said, unimpressed by Cocó's argument. "You might recall that after the Machado dictatorship, the economy was a mess for the next five years and land prices dropped dramatically. I don't expect that it will be any different this time."

Tony could tell that Cocó was starting to get agitated. He

did not like being contradicted, especially not by his son-in-law because Victor de la Torre, the beneficiary of a liberal education at Yale, was usually very well informed. Every time they argued about history, economics or almost any topic, it was clear to Tony that his father knew more about the topic and won all the arguments. However, that Sunday, Cocó pulled out his trump card.

"Victor, if you are so smart, how come you don't have a job right now? What has all your education gotten you? How come you have to live in my house?"

Everyone at the table froze. Tony thought it was a fair question, the part about the job, but it seemed impolite to point that out in front of the entire family. But the part about staying in his house was uncalled for. It was still common for daughters and even sons of wealthy patriarchs to remain in their parents' houses, like in the old days. He had even heard that his father's generation was unusual because that group had a large number of wealthy women in it, whereas the men were not as wealthy. When the men married those women, they didn't have too many incentives to be ambitious and work hard to build their own houses and stock them with servants. Their wives' parents had large houses with plenty of extra rooms.

Still, Tony felt sorry for his father, who did not have an answer to the part about not having a job. In all fairness, when Don Antonio sold La Estrella in the late forties and the entire de la Torre family moved to Havana, his father did try some business ideas, but they all seemed to fail. He tried drilling for oil with some of his friends from the Country Club, but the oil they found was too low grade. With another group of friends, they tried to make pre-fabricated housing, using *bagazo*, the leftovers from the sugar process, but that did not take. Apparently, the pre-fabricated walls had a funny smell. They had even experimented with a restaurant chain that only served chicken, and customers ordered from the car window. It flopped. His father had tried to make money, but he did not seem to have a flair for business. Now he was mostly playing golf and bridge—and he had a flair for those games—until some other business idea took hold.

His dad stared at Cocó briefly, poker faced, after Coco's impolite remark, then lowered his glance and concentrated on his lobster. Tony noticed how Cocó seemed highly pleased with his statement, and how it seemed to end the argument in his favor. Cocó dug into his lobster with gusto. José Ignacio entered the dining room and started clearing the plates. Shortly afterward he brought a tray of *flans*. Rolando's *flans* were famous in Havana society. It was the perfect mood changer, as everyone made sounds of approval of Rolando's choice of dessert.

After lunch, Tony went to his room. He liked to nap after a big lunch. Usually he turned on the radio, found the latest song by Benny Moré or Rolando LaSerie and fell asleep. That day he was too restless. He felt bad for his dad, although he knew that his dad was no angel, and in fact, deserved all he got from Cocó. Not only did his father not work enough, but he drank too much scotch and did not spend enough time with his wife and his children. Not often, but on days like this one, he wished his father had a normal job. He wished his father was a moneymaker and had his own house.

On the other hand, maybe making money was not an important issue in his father's life because, Tony assumed, his father's family had always had money. The de la Torres had owned sugar mills for generations. Money on that side of the family was a given, not something that they ever worried about, aspired to have or talked about at the dinner table. Maybe his father didn't have money because making money, in his father's world-view, was not a worthy goal in life. Having fun was more what he had in mind. If his father valued anything, Tony guessed, it was his friends, his brothers and how well a person played bridge and golf. But the real key to membership in his father's group was a sense of humor. They had to be simpatico. They had to know how to tell a good story. They could be thieves. They could be bankrupt. But they could not be bores.

That could all be true, but Tony could easily take Cocó side. He had to admit that on the big issues, Cocó always came through. He always rehired Rolando and waived the advances he was owed. All the other servants were loyal to him, including Gonzalo. Cocó became furious every time Tony's grandmother or his mother overwhelmed Gonzalo with too many errands. He also gave Tony's mother a generous allowance, so she was never short of money for herself or her children. Also, he was going to pay for Tony's Choate education and Choate was not cheap. That last item was particularly admirable since Cocó did not seem to have a high opinion about the benefits of a Choate education. Tony's father had gone to Choate.

Cocó had a right to be upset with Tony's dad. Not only was Victor an insufficient provider, Tony could attest to the fact that he was not a terrific father either, simply because he was never around. Tony's mother had been more present, especially when he was younger, although now she had a busy life in the goings-on of Havana society.

The adults, *la gente grande*, as the children called them, seemed to live in a separate world, separate from the children, and he could tell that it was the same at his cousins' houses. His contact with adults was mostly with the servants: First with his nanny Graciela when he was young, then with the male servants.

When Tony was not hanging out and getting his sexual education with Gonzalo, he was getting boxing lessons from Rolando, who had been a professional boxer as a young man or getting a malt made for him by José Ignacio, the butler. The servants raised him. This was not unusual in well-to-do Havana households. What was unusual was that Tony could not remember ever having had a conversation with his father that lasted for more than a few minutes.

Still, he liked his father. He admired all the things he had done, all the funny stories he told at the dinner table and how everyone in Havana liked him. Tony was always introduced to adults as Victor de la Torre's son, *el hijo de Victor*, and because of that fact, they all seemed to like him, too. In Cuba, all was forgiven if you could make people laugh. Tony often wished he was as funny as his father or could tell as good a story.

His father's routine was a good one. El Gordo Ramos, one of his golfing friends, picked him up every morning. They spent the day at the Havana Country Club. They golfed in the morning, ate lunch at the Club and later in the afternoon, the other de la Torre brothers would show up. His de la Torre uncles were harder workers than his father; at least, they had an office to go to. But still, after work, they all ended up at the Country Club, ready to play bridge into the night and drink scotch.

What Tony liked the most about the four de la Torre brothers was how well they got along. It was obvious that they loved each other. Why not? They had spent a charmed childhood together, growing up first on Amargura Street, and later, at La Estrella, where the brothers hunted, rode horses and went on three-day fishing trips in Don Antonio's two-masted schooner. They had even better times as young men at Choate and Yale. They were outstanding athletes and played together on the same teams. They were rich, smart, good looking and the girls were all over them. The stories his dad told about all the crazy things they did in St. Elmo's, their Yale fraternity, were amusing and outrageous. They brought their entire fraternity back to Havana one spring vacation, and Tony could imagine what went on every night when they hit the nightclubs, the bars and undoubtedly, the brothels.

When the brothers graduated from Yale, they continued the good times in Havana, attending Havana society parties as available and highly desirable bachelors.

Then the de la Torres all got married. Now all the brothers had their own families and their own family troubles. But they quickly figured out that they could not bear staying apart, so they met at the Country Club, golfed as often as possible and played bridge at night. Food and drinks were brought over to their tables; they told stories, they laughed raucously, they ordered more drinks, they told more stories, and when the brothers teamed up, they usually won at all the games they played. Tony had heard that the de la Torre brothers were the best bridge players in Cuba. They were the top golfers, too.

Tony vaguely understood that his father could not close the chapter on his childhood, on his original family unit, on a life of fun, locker rooms and games. Life with his new family was not nearly as much fun as the life he had lived with his brothers, so he held on to that other life.

At night, around nine, Tony would ride with his mother to pick up his dad at the Country Club. On the way over, he liked listening to his mother's gossip about her friends. His mother was usually in very high spirits. She was a survivor. All the women married to the de la Torre brothers had to be.

But then, at the club, his father would make them wait twenty, thirty minutes in the car, while he finished his bridge hand or his drink. His mother often got upset after a long wait, and his parents would argue and then drive back without saying a word. Tony hated those arguments, their long silences and how his father seemed to be insensitive toward his mother. But he still liked going on those car trips. On the trip back, he loved to roll down the windows in the back seat of his father's Mercury, take in the breeze and the sweet fragrance of all the jasmine planted in the flowerbeds along Miramar's Fifth Avenue and fall asleep.

He felt sorry for his mother, but she told Tony, more than once, that no matter how many problems she had with his dad, he was still the love of her life. Nothing was ever going to change that. His mom was like one of those animals that he read about in his zoology book, who mated for life. When she said the "till death" part of her vows, she meant it.

Tony knew that his mother could have married anyone. In all the pictures of his mother taken before her marriage, Tony could see that she was very beautiful, and her family had plenty of money.

Now his mother kept very busy. During the day, she had a non-stop schedule of shopping, lunches, canasta parties and golf lessons. On the weekends, there were parties and dinners. Then there was Sofi. His older sister was about to become a debutante, and the party, scheduled for October at the Havana Yacht Club, required extensive planning. And more importantly, Sofi had to be outfitted with clothes, social graces and the correct posture. His mother, like the other women in his family, was a great believer in appearances and performing well in society. Everything about Sofi's debutante party had to be perfect.

There was one benefit to his mother's focus on Sofi and his father's absence: no one was paying much attention to Tony.

Tony was aware that he could do whatever he pleased.

8

THE FOLLOWING WEEK, TONY wondered if Emilio was going to invite him to lunch again. Maybe Emilio had decided that anyone who hadn't kissed an American girl, had never heard of Porfirio Rubirosa and didn't have a Rolex watch to throw out of windows was a *guajiro*, a country hick. But it seemed that they were destined to be close friends since they were both going to the same American school in the fall.

Considering how they met, and after watching his performance at El Encanto, Tony knew that being friends with Emilio was also going to lead to trouble. Still, he felt drawn to him. Tony had always been a good boy, done well at school and behaved properly. But now, he sensed an opportunity to be bad.

Emilio was definitely bad, especially when it came to dealing with girls. Tony was intrigued by the possibility of meeting some local American girls. Maybe Emilio would take him to an American teenage party in the Biltmore section.

Tony also enjoyed riding around Havana in Emilio's white Mercedes. When Tony rode in his family's black Cadillac, not many people noticed. Chauffeur-driven black Cadillacs were a common sight in Havana. Every family he knew had one. A white Mercedes, however, stood out. There were only two or three in Havana. When he and Emilio were riding in that car, everyone on the street and in other cars stared at them.

When Tony returned home from school one day, he considered calling Emilio to invite him to lunch at his house on a Saturday. But he thought that the conversation at his family's table would not be too interesting. His grandmother, mother and aunt would carry on about the party they had attended the previous night. They would discuss what had been served and who looked awful. His grandfather and his father might argue again. Tony stared at the phone for a while.

Tony did not think he was good at initiating anything. He suffered from inertia. He decided that it was easier to leave it up to Emilio. If Emilio called again, he would go along with whatever Emilio proposed. But if he didn't call, that would be okay, too.

The person Tony really wanted to call was his cousin Tina. Tina and Carmen talked about everything. He wanted to ask Tina if Carmen had said anything to her about him.

After he saw Carmen getting a tan at the Yacht Club, he couldn't stop thinking about her. Was she the girl destined to be his girlfriend and someday his wife? He hoped so. Was it fate that had brought them together last summer for such a terrific vacation at his uncle's ranch? Why was Carmen there and not someone else? That had to be destiny at work.

Now he wanted to find out if Tina and Carmen were going to Ciego for another stay at the ranch when the summer started. If they were going, he would invite himself, which would not be a problem because he got along very well with Tina's mom and dad. He could look forward to more swims in the river with Carmen on hot summer nights.

But he didn't call Tina either. Tina would tease him about his interest in Carmen, and she would surely tell Carmen about his call. And if Tina's mother heard of the call, she would also tease Tony about it. Tía Nina was a real teaser, too. And Tina's mother and Carmen's mother had grown up together, so Carmen's mother would also be in the loop. The whole thing would get out of control and turn into a disaster. It was better not to call Tina.

TONY woke up that night in the middle of an orgasm. As soon as he realized what had happened, that he had been immersed in a dream and not real life, he felt terribly disappointed.

In his dream, he was older and had married Carmen. The dream had started at the wedding. Tony had been thinking during the entire ceremony about later that night when they would make love for the first time.

Then the dream moved on to their room at the Hotel Nacional, Havana's best hotel. Their room had a large balcony overlooking the Caribbean Sea. They had champagne on the balcony. They were both a little giddy.

Then he was waiting for her in bed. He was nervous because he was still a virgin. Carmen was also a virgin, even more nervous. She was in the bathroom. When the bathroom door opened, he was excited to see that Carmen was wearing a sexy white satin slip, fitted tightly to her body. As she approached the bed, her mood changed. Her smile seemed to say: this is going to be fun!

She moved on to the bed, and they started kissing. Soon they were making love with such passion and such pleasure that everyone staying on their floor in the Hotel Nacional must have heard their love groans.

9

ON SUNDAY MORNING HE LEARNED
from Gonzalo that the family was going to the twelve o'clock mass
at the Corpus Christi church. Tony liked that plan because Emilio's
house was a few blocks uphill from the church, and he guessed
that he might run into Emilio there. Tina and Carmen Maciá also
lived in that section. His family knew everyone who went to that
mass. The scene outside the church after every Sunday mass was
almost like a cocktail party, except without cocktails.

There was another reason why Tony liked going to Corpus
Christi: It was so crowded on Sundays that only the women and
children got to sit inside. The men and the older boys stood in
the back of the church and spilled over outside. Spilling outside is
what Tony liked to do.

Corpus Cristi was the first large Havana church with air conditioning, a big plus for those inside in the summer, although he missed watching the little performance his grandmother did with her fan in all the other churches. She moved her wrist in a certain way, flicked the fan open, fanned herself about five times and flicked it close. Within seconds, she would repeat the cycle. Tony's grandmother wore a charm bracelet on her wrist, with many gold trinkets hanging from it, and when she fanned herself, her jewelry jingled loudly. She liked that sound. At Corpus Christi, Tony's grandmother was uncharacteristically quiet because the air conditioning didn't give her a reason to work her fan there.

Whenever he sat inside, he enjoyed watching the girls his age. Lots of attractive girls went to that church. They looked good wearing white veils and pastel dresses that hugged their waists and revealed their fine figures. He especially enjoyed watching them when they made their way back to their seats after they took communion. They looked so serious, having just taken in the body of Christ, their hands clasped in a prayer position right against their breasts, trying to hold back their breasts or hide them. But it was hopeless. Some of those girls had terrific breasts.

The women in his family, like the other women in the church, were very religious. Tony's mother, his older sister, his grandmother and his aunt had communion every Sunday, and they prayed during the mass. For them, religion was serious business. The men were another story. Some men had communion, but not many.

Tony never had communion. To have communion, his soul had to be free of sins, even venial sins like swearing, not to mention the more serious sins, like masturbation. Between Friday, when he had confession at Belén, and Sunday, when he went to mass, Tony would have masturbated at least four times, would have sworn every time he talked to Gonzalo and would have had at least a few hundred bad thoughts meander through his mind. In case there was a hell, he was not going to risk having communion with his soul replete with sins.

When the men arrived, they first went inside with their families. As the church filled up, the men seated inside politely gave up their seats to the newly arrived women. They headed for the back, stood there for a short while and then sneaked out. There was a large terrace by the front portal of the church where the men would clump in groups and carry on spirited conversations, sometimes about politics or business, but more often about the golf game they had played the day before. Men seemed to be more focused on this world.

That Sunday, Tony decided to sit inside and look at the girls. He was hoping he could watch Carmen walk back from communion, working at holding her breasts back, but for some reason, she didn't have communion that day. When the mass ended, he went outside and quickly spotted Ramiro with a group of his de la Torre cousins. He joined them. Ramiro was predictable—he was bragging about how he was going to win the champion bat title for his baseball league. Right behind his group of cousins, Tony could see that his father and his three brothers were already arguing. They would pick a topic, any topic, and then they would start arguing, often about how badly one of them had played a bridge hand. But the arguments never got heated. Usually, no more than three or four sentences were uttered before the four brothers broke out laughing.

Someone tapped Tony on the back. It was Emilio. He didn't waste any time: "Do you want to come over for lunch next Saturday?"

"Sure," Tony said. He was pleased to be invited again.

"I've got a special day planned," he said, smiling. Then he left. Tony did not know how to interpret that parting statement.

He did not know whether he should look forward to the following Saturday or start worrying. The way Emilio had grinned told Tony that he should start worrying. He could picture a blackboard equation: Emilio equals trouble. But he could also picture another equation: Emilio equals adventures with girls.

As the church emptied, the gathering on the front terrace turned into a full-blown social event. Everyone lingered, greeted each other, kissed and shook hands as the volume of the conversations on the terrace increased steadily. Tony started making the rounds, kissing his aunts and his older girl cousins on their cheeks. It got confusing at times—whom to kiss. It was clear he should kiss his aunts and his mother's friends, but was he supposed to kiss his girl cousins his age and their girl friends, too?

He heard a familiar voice: *"Oráculo, como estás!"* It was Tía Nina, Tina's mother. She called him the Oracle because her son Luis, who was younger than Tony, was always saying to her that Tony said this and Tony said that. She concluded that Tony must be the Oracle. She liked to kid with him, and Tony did not mind. She offered her cheek to him, bending down a little, and he kissed her. Tina was with her, and he kissed her too. Next to Tina was Carmen Maciá, the girl he had married in his dream the night before. He decided to be reckless. He also kissed Carmen on her cheek.

"I dreamt about you last night," Tony blurted out, almost as if someone else was inside of him, saying things. He had not planned to say that.

"Tony de la Torre! Please!" Carmen appeared surprised and embarrassed, but she laughed.

"It was just a dream, and you were in it," Tony said, enjoying his newfound boldness. He could tell Carmen was interested.

"Since you've started this ridiculous conversation, you now have to tell me what the dream was about."

"It's embarrassing."

Tina and Carmen shrieked. Some families nearby stared at them.

"Now I really want to hear it," Carmen said, laughing again.

"I dreamt that we got married."

Carmen laughed again.

"Tony," she said. "I would not call your dream embarrassing. I would call it improbable."

"You cannot predict the future, Carmen."

He noticed that Carmen looked pleased, and it was not something he was imagining because she wanted to know more.

"And where did we go on our honeymoon? It better be an exciting place!"

He better not tell her that they had gone to the Hotel Nacional, right there in the Vedado district.

"We went to Tahiti." That should be an adequate honeymoon, Tony thought.

"How mundane," Carmen said. "What I have in mind is a trip around the world."

Carmen probably meant it, Tony thought. She was the type of girl who had high expectations. Why not? She was attractive and smart. Not that a honeymoon trip around the world was out of the question. His de la Torre grandfather had done it. Don Antonio and Otrín, his other grandmother, traveled around the world for their honeymoon in 1905. Otrín told him that what surprised her about that trip was that most countries they went to, including Spain, had no electricity. They even went to China.

Tony's mother, sister and grandmother joined their group, and Tina and Carmen started to kiss them. Their arrival ended any further discussion about Tony's dream, which was a relief. If she asked more questions, he would have to lie some more, and he was not a convincing liar. More relatives joined them. Like a flock of parrots, within minutes, the noise level in their group, and in the other groups around them, reached a crescendo. Then, as if socializing after mass had reached an agreed upon time limit, all the women on the terrace started kissing each other profusely. Men shook hands with other men, and the entire congregation headed for their cars and their lunch destinations.

10

TONY HAD BEEN LOOKING FORWARD
to another lunch at the Eloys', and he was not disappointed.
Emilio's father was in his usual upbeat and talkative mood. He
seemed incapable of talking about trivial topics, like gossip or
funny stories about acquaintances, which were the preferred din-
nertime topics at Tony's home.

The Eloys and Tony sat down at the table. Within minutes,
Mr. Eloy was carrying on about the importance of courage and not
being afraid of anything. Then, surprising Tony, he started reciting
the poem, *The Charge of the Light Brigade*. Mr. Eloy, who had
taught himself English, spoke it well. He recited the poem with
excellent diction and some dramatic skill:

> *Cannon to right of them,*
> *Cannon to left of them,*

Cannon in front of them
Volley'd and thunder'd;
Storm'd at with shot and shell,
Boldly they rode and well,
Into the jaws of Death,
Into the mouth of Hell
Rode the six hundred.

The fate of the Light Brigade did not strike Tony as a very good example of the benefits of acting courageously, but then Mr. Eloy explained how he used this poem as an inspiration during the early days of his insurance company. In those days, he waged a daily business battle against bigger foes, charging them head on, without fear, like the cavalry officers in the poem. He had never been afraid to tackle insurmountable odds, and that attitude paid off. Fear was not a word in his vocabulary.

He recounted a story when he was starting in business, trying to sell insurance in Holguín, in Oriente Province. At the time, he was not succeeding at getting new clients. At night, to relax, he went to the local pool hall to play pool. One night, he was playing a winning game, and some men were watching. Among them were the town bully, a big guy and a small-time hood. He made some derogatory remarks about the insurance salesman from Havana. Mr. Eloy ignored the first few remarks, but then he distinctly heard him say: "The little midget thinks he's a snappy dresser." That proved to be an unfortunate comment.

In those days, Mr. Eloy always wore a white shirt and a bow tie, American style. He was proud how well he dressed, and he was sensitive about his stature. He very calmly walked up to the bully and broke the thick part of his cue stick on his head, knocking him out. The next day, he started selling insurance in Holguín.

"Dad has punched out a lot of people," Emilio said, with considerable pride in his voice.

"That's true," Mr. Eloy said, laughing. "I have a temper, and I've been known to get into a few fights, but I'm not proud of it. But enough talk about me. I want to know more about you, Tony. Tell me, what are you interested in?"

That question surprised Tony. Adults were never interested in the details of his life, except for the priests. Tony wasn't sure how to answer. Girls? His fantasy life? Sports was a safe answer.

"I play some baseball, but I'm not very good at it. Mostly, I like to fish."

"How about school? What classes interest you?" Mr. Eloy was not going to let him off the hook.

"I'm good at math and science, but I like history."

"I'm distressingly ignorant when it comes to math and science, but today, those subjects are very important. Good for you. I wish Emilio paid more attention to those subjects and to his other subjects, as well. Now, history, that is very important. I share that interest with you. I'm interested in men who have made history. Reading biographies is one of my hobbies. I have learned much from great men."

"Dad," Emilio said. "Don't worry about me. Next year I'm going to be an excellent student. I'm going to work hard, and Tony is going to help me. By the way, we plan to go to the movies after lunch to see the John Wayne movie at the Miramar."

The John Wayne movie was not playing at the Miramar, Tony thought.

"Emilio, dear," his mother said. "You know your father and I feel it's important that you take your studies seriously."

But Mr. Eloy did not want to talk about Emilio's studies. He was still focused on Tony. He wanted to know about his family. He said that he did not know his father and uncles that well, but he knew his de la Torre grandfather well. How was Don Antonio?

"He's retired now, but he's fine." Tony said.

Tony found it interesting how everyone called his de la Torre grandfather Don Antonio, an honorific title given to some men, usually older men, but not to everyone. The Don was a title that had to be earned. The curious thing about his grandfather was that he had been called Don Antonio the moment he turned thirty.

"When Don Antonio owned La Estrella, Eloy Insurance had the insurance contract with the sugar mill," Mr. Eloy said. "Your grandfather is a delightful person, a pleasure to do business with and one of the great men in the Cuban sugar industry."

"Yes," Tony said. "I like my grandfather a lot. He taught me how to fish."

"Tell me about that," Mr. Eloy said.

Mr. Eloy continued to impress Tony, especially how he seemed genuinely interested in the details of his life. He told him about the fishing trips at La Estrella. His grandfather kept an old 70-foot two-masted schooner anchored at a beach, 30 minutes by jeep from the sugar mill. The boat was originally built to transport charcoal from Cayo Romano to the mainland. His grandfather had the boat cleaned, painted, and a new and perfectly equipped kitchen was built in the cabin.

Tony remembered having some wonderful dinners at sea—nothing tastes as good as a fish that goes straight from the ocean into the frying pan. Over the open hold, a canvas roof was designed to hang from the bottom spar of the main mast to protect the family from the sun and rain. The boat was large enough to accommodate up to 25 people on three-day weekend trips: Don Antonio, his sons and their wives, guests from Havana, the five or six oldest grandchildren, the captain, the cook and, often, a trio of local musicians who played guitar and sang *boleros*.

They sailed to the many unpopulated islands north of Camaguey Province. At the islands, they snorkeled for lobster, bottom fished from the boat, went swimming on deserted sandy beaches with crystal clear water. At sunset they anchored in protected coves, ate seafood dinners while the trio played, then slept in canvas beds set up on the hold. Often they took the cots to the island on the dinghy and would sleep on the beach. It was wonderful, falling asleep in the ocean breeze under a canopy of stars. Tony loved those trips.

He didn't tell Mr. Eloy that every time the family returned to the sugar mill from the fishing trips, he would run up to his bedroom, lock himself in and cry. He couldn't bear the thought that the trip had ended.

"A trio playing boleros! Now that's what I call fishing in style!" Mr. Eloy exclaimed. "What a delightful story. You will never forget those days. There is nothing that can compare to growing up close to nature. There weren't many fishing trips in my childhood."

Then Mr. Eloy told his story. He started selling insurance right after high school, and he quickly found out he was very good at it. He was good at it because he could explain with clear logic to a prospective client what a good deal life insurance was. No one understood that. He believed in his product. That was the key. He had a lot of energy in those days, driving all over the island selling insurance in small towns. There were no hotels in those towns so he slept in his car. He could write a book about what he learned, about people, about business and about perseverance. Above all, he learned to believe in himself and to trust his instincts about people.

Then he got going again on Bernard Baruch. He told a long

story about how Bernard Baruch had amassed a fortune by refusing to go along with the crowd. When everyone was speculating and buying stocks in the late Twenties, Bernard Baruch recognized that a speculative bubble was forming and sold all his holdings. Then, when investors were selling all their stocks for close to nothing in the early Thirties, Bernard was busy buying them back. Ten years later he was one of the richest men in America.

"These are the lessons of Bernard Baruch, boys," Mr. Eloy concluded. "Strike your course in life, be an individual—that's what the American spirit is all about. Disregard what others think, never go along with the herd, hold your course, believe in honor, revere courage. It's very simple."

That was a mouthful, Tony thought. He wondered if Mr. Eloy knew what a small dent the lessons of Bernard Baruch had made on his son, who made it a habit to terrorize boys at locker rooms and female store clerks at bra counters. But maybe the lessons had sunk in. Emilio had a total disregard for conventional behavior; he did what he pleased; he was fearless. The honor part, though, seemed to be missing.

Tony could tell that Emilio's father loved having an audience and thrived on it. Mrs. Eloy listened with full attention to everything Mr. Eloy said. Tony could tell how much she admired him. Emilio paid attention at times, but at other times, he did not. Tony was a very good audience. Mr. Eloy, a self-made millionaire, had earned the right to lecture him all he wanted.

Listening to Mr. Eloy felt different from listening to his grandfather Cocó, who also talked about his business. But Cocó's activities, based on sugar and cattle, belonged to the past. Money had always been made in Cuba by working the land. Mr. Eloy was more in tune with the future. His insurance business was about the modern world and about advertising. Tony liked how he was interested in passing down what he knew about life. Mr. Eloy was a philosopher specializing in the philosophy of success.

Tony was interested in Mr. Eloy's advice because he worried about his future. He couldn't see it too clearly. All he knew was that the de la Torre family had a tradition of wealth, and he wanted to continue that tradition. Not being wealthy did not seem to be an option. If he were not wealthy, not one of the girls he knew would fall in love with him, starting with Carmen Macía. He also wanted to have his own house on Varadero Beach and continue to spend his summers there with his future family.

The problem was that he could not foresee how he was going to become wealthy. He had to excel at something to create wealth. The question was: in what field? Tony could not imagine what profession he had skills for or what interested him. He couldn't see himself as a successful businessman. He would never be aggressive enough to break cue sticks on people's heads or charming enough to sell them products they didn't need. The boys he knew did not worry about their futures—they were going to take over their fathers' businesses. Emilio had already mentioned he was going to work for Seguros Eloy. Why not? His father had founded the company, and now his father dreamed of the day when his son could take over after he retired.

After lunch, they went for a ride in the Mercedes. When they got in the car, Emilio said: "I've planned a surprise."

"What's the surprise?" Tony asked.

"You'll see."

Tony thought that this was a habit of Emilio he did not like. Emilio didn't offer options. He didn't ask. He made plans and assumed that Tony would gladly go along. On the other hand, maybe Emilio's habits were the habits of highly successful men, like Mr. Eloy, like Bernard Baruch. They didn't ask. They laid out the course of action. It seemed like he could learn life lessons every time he was around the Eloys.

Tony hoped that Roberto would fork to the left after they passed the Corpus Christi church and head toward the Biltmore area, where the American families lived in Havana. Instead, he turned to the right, toward Miramar. He could not think of anything exciting they could do in Miramar except go to the movies, but that was not likely. Then Roberto crossed the river into the Vedado and took the two-lane highway to Rancho Boyeros, the airport. There was only one interesting thing to do in that neighborhood besides going on a trip abroad. Tony started to suspect they were going to the Mambo Club. He asked Emilio if that was the surprise.

"Yes," he said, beaming.

Tony panicked. Somehow, he had not anticipated that they would be going to the Mambo so soon. But he did not want to appear nervous or fearful. He wanted to impress Emilio. Being a coward was not on the list of character traits that the Eloys admired. He had to adopt a "Charge of the Light Brigade" attitude.

"Okay," Tony finally said.

But it was not okay. When Tony thought about having sex, he mostly thought about what could go wrong. Would he know what to do? Was his penis too small? Maybe it was too small to reach the vagina—and where was that? He was not too clear about the female anatomy or the physical maneuvers involved in lovemaking. What if the woman he went in with had crabs? He had also heard that one should not have sex after lunch. He could get deadly cramps. If he survived the cramps and the crabs, he could still get syphilis and die a horrible death, like his great aunt Margarita. Besides, he did not have ten dollars.

"I don't have ten dollars," Tony blurted out.

"I'm treating," Emilio said, handing him the money.

He could not think of another objection. They were silent for a while. Then he thought that going to the Mambo had a positive side. Lately, it was becoming obvious this was something he had to do, like having his baby teeth pulled. And it was better that he do it sooner rather than later, at the Mambo instead of Barrio Colón or Marina.

"Are you nervous?" Emilio said.

"No," Tony lied.

"Well, I am," Emilio said, laughing.

"Okay. I'm nervous, too," Tony admitted.

"We'll have a drink first, " Emilio said. "A drink will relax us."

"Sure, a drink is a good idea."

Tony had sneaked a few drinks at family parties, just to try them. He did not like the taste of anything he tried, although he enjoyed getting dizzy. He especially could not understand why his father liked Scotch. He nearly threw up the first time he tried Scotch. Dark rum was not too bad.

The Mambo Club did not look like much from the outside, a boxy one level stucco building with a large orange neon sign on the roof that flashed the club's name on and off. Inside, it looked more spacious and more prosperous. There was a trio playing, a small dance floor, tables around the dance floor and a long mahogany bar to one side. Relatively well-dressed young women were sitting in small groups at the bar and at the tables near the dance floor. It looked like a normal place. But Tony soon noticed how couples were exiting and returning through a back door.

Tony was relieved to notice that no one paid much attention to him. Age limits in brothels did not exist. They found a table by the dance floor and quickly ordered two rum and cokes. Tony looked around. They had the distinction of being the only thirteen-year-old boys there. The other customers were mostly middle-aged men.

It must have been obvious that it was their first time at a brothel because a few minutes had barely passed before two women sat down on their table and started kidding with them. Was this their first time? The one who sat next to Tony said that she could tell he was a little nervous, but he didn't need to worry because her specialty was breaking in young boys. Her name was Sylvia, and she assured Tony that if he did it with her, his first time would go smoothly. She was very pale, and her hair was bleached blond. She was going for the Marilyn look.

Tony had no idea how he was supposed to talk to a prostitute, so he listened to Sylvia. What she said about being a first-time specialist interested him. She suggested they dance. They got up and moved to the dance floor.

Sylvia danced very close. This was not how the girls in his group were going to dance at the summer parties on Varadero Beach. The official rule there was that a twelve-inch ruler should fit between couples. In the old days, one of the chaperones went around the dance floor checking couples with the ruler.

Sylvia not only danced close, but she also started grinding her pelvis against Tony's, to the rhythm of the cha-cha-chá. Sylvia separated a little: "You are a very good dancer," she said, smiling. Then she moved close again, their faces cheek-to-cheek, and she continued rhythmically grinding away, cha-cha-chá, cha-cha-chá. She moved apart once more: "I'm looking forward to making love to you." She moved closer again, cha-cha-chá, cha-cha-chá.

It did not take long for Tony to become a fan of the cha-cha-chá. It took even less time to get an erection. Sylvia could feel it too.

She separated and looked down: "I think you are ready to go in!" she said, laughing.

Tony was embarrassed, but there was no denying that he was aroused. He might as well do it with Sylvia—a first time specialist.

He glanced toward Emilio. He was dancing, too, and Tony noticed that Emilio's partner was giving him the same treatment—the pelvic grind and dancing cheek-to-cheek. Emilio was grinning, his eyes closed. When the song ended, Emilio came up to Tony.

"I'm going in," he said.

Tony did not hesitate. "I'm going in, too."

They walked with their partners to the back of the club, where an older woman sat on a stool by the door and collected ten dollars from every customer. Emilio paid and went in first. Then Tony gave the woman the 10 dollars that Emilio had given him and followed Sylvia down a corridor.

They entered a sparsely furnished room with a gigantic mirror set on the ceiling over the bed. He had never seen a mirror in that location before, but he could guess why it was there. The moment Sylvia closed the door, she turned into a different person—a very efficient businesswoman. She undressed rather quickly, helped Tony out of his clothes and led Tony to the bed. What happened next happened very fast. Sylvia was into fast turnovers. They had barely talked and within a few minutes he was inside her—Sylvia had guided him in with her hand—and ten seconds later, he came.

"Oh!" Sylvia said. Even the first-time specialist was surprised.

"That was very nice, sweetie," she said. "You can get dressed now. I'm going to stay here to tidy the room a bit."

What was that all about? Tony thought. After years of sexual fantasies, bad thoughts and high expectations, that was it? It seemed to him that the whole business of sex had been highly overrated.

And even worse, he suspected he had proven to be a flop as a lover. He was the world's only ten-second lover. He dressed as quickly as possible, politely said thank you and left the room. On the way back to his table, he thought he probably broke the record for the fastest ten dollars ever made at the Mambo Club.

He sat down at their table and ordered another Cuba Libre. When the drink arrived, he gulped it down and tried to think about what had happened. He couldn't think too clearly, so he ordered a third Cuba Libre.

Then everything cleared up. He thought his first time wasn't a complete disaster. He was no longer a virgin. He had done it! Everything had functioned more or less normally, perhaps too fast, but he didn't need to go into the details. Now Gonzalo could relax—his mission accomplished—and his cousin Ramiro would not be able to tease him anymore.

When Emilio returned, twenty minutes later, he also ordered another Cuba Libre. He wanted to toast to their new stage in life.

"How did it go?" Emilio asked, grinning.

"Really well!" Tony replied.

ON the ride back, Emilio couldn't stop talking. He obviously enjoyed his first time. The woman he did it with was incredibly sexy. He could not wait to go in with her again. He asked Tony when he was leaving for Varadero Beach. Emilio wanted to plan as many trips as possible to the Mambo before Tony left for the beach and before Emilio left with his parents for another European trip.

"Classes end next week," Tony said. "We can go next weekend. Then my family leaves for the beach the following Wednesday." Tony figured they would go once more, after another Saturday lunch at the Eloys'. Then he would put his brothel career on hold. Maybe going to brothels would be more interesting when he was older.

Emilio thought for a moment.

"Okay! Let's go tomorrow, Sunday and next Saturday and next Sunday, and we'll go on your last Tuesday night and have a farewell party. How's that?"

"Okay." What the hell, Tony thought. Go for it! Maybe it will get better.

They agreed to meet at the Yacht Club the following day and go after lunch. Emilio told Tony he was going to do it with the same woman. She had let him do it twice. Did he do it twice?

Tony decided not to lie. "No, I only did it once, and then she kicked me out of the room."

"Tomorrow," Emilio said. "Make it clear that you want to do it twice. I thought you knew that. Everyone knows that at the Mambo, for ten dollars, you get to do it twice."

11

ON SUNDAY MORNING, TONY AND Gonzalo went out on foot to get freshly baked bread on 23rd Street. They were walking up G Street when he told Gonzalo about the Mambo the night before. Gonzalo was delighted. He stopped walking and shook Tony's hand.

"Congratulations! Now you are a man!"

"This is a little embarrassing, but I have a question. It all happened very fast. "

Gonzalo laughed. They continued walking.

"You mean, you came very fast. Don't worry about that," he said. "What's important is to do it as often as possible."

"I'm serious. Is that normal?"

"It's normal if you are thirteen. You learn to control it. Women take longer than men to feel sexual pleasure, so if you are going to please a woman, you have to slow down."

"So how do I slow down?"

"Practice. You've got to practice, like you practice hitting a baseball. You take a lot of swings at practice to get good at hitting. It's the same for sex. Keep going to the Mambo."

"So what do I do the next time?"

"Try this. When you feel you are going to come, think about something else, something that has nothing to do with sex, like the ideal lineup for the Havana baseball club."

"I know very well what the ideal lineup should be. That won't take me too much time."

"Then think of whom they should trade for."

"Okay."

THEY went to the noon mass at Corpus Christi again. Tony decided to sit inside with his mother and sisters and enjoy the air-conditioning. He went through the choreography of attending mass—standing up, sitting down, kneeling, sometimes with his hands in a prayer position. He must have looked like a model boy and a perfect Catholic, but all he could think about was his disaster at the Mambo. He wondered if the mothers piously praying in this church had any idea that their thirteen-year-old sons were all going to brothels. The fathers knew. They grew up in Havana.

It bothered him to think how much Emilio enjoyed his first time, while he had been so disappointed. He was also starting to worry about this new turn of events—it looked like Emilio would want to go to a brothel every time they got together. He wondered what happened in Emilio's room that excited him so much. He didn't go into much detail on the ride home, only that the woman he did it with *estaba buenísima*, and they got along gloriously. And of course, that they did it twice.

Sylvia didn't turn out to be a very good first-time specialist. On

his next brothel excursion, he planned on selecting someone interested in talking. Someone who was not in a big rush. He wanted to
feel as enthused as Emilio about going to the Mambo again.

After mass, his family lingered again by the front of the church.
He found Tina and Carmen. Carmen asked him, laughing, had he
had any more interesting dreams lately? He came up with an inadequate answer. He said no. Later, he replayed Carmen's playful
question with a string of possible playful answers. His lame answer
had been an opportunity lost, but he had made up for his lapse by
asking Carmen about her summer plans.

"Tina has invited me to stay most of the summer with her family in Varadero, and I managed to convince my mother to let me
do it. My mother has to stay in Havana to teach a summer class
at the university. I'm looking forward to a summer on the beach."

"I'll be seeing you there, then," Tony said.

"Yes, I'm sure you will," Carmen said, smiling.

On the drive to the Yacht Club, he couldn't help feeling excited by what Carmen had said and how she had smiled when
she said it. She had been sure that he would be seeing her on the
beach. That had to mean something. The beach for him had always
meant fishing, snorkeling and water skiing. He was in the water
most of the day. This summer he would add visiting Carmen to
the list.

As they had planned, he met up with Emilio at the Yacht
Club. Emilio's parents never came with him. They preferred to
stay home on weekends. Mr. Eloy undoubtedly thought that the
goings-on of Havana society were a waste of time. He was too
busy building a financial empire and reading books about Bernard
Baruch. One immediate benefit of Mr. Eloy's antisocial behavior was that Emilio had Roberto and the white Mercedes at his
disposal.

The moment his family finished lunch, Emilio walked up to their table with his signature smile and proceeded to kiss his mother, aunt and grandmother. He shook hands with all the men. He was socially adept and polite. It was clear that adults did not intimidate him, and they liked him for it. They left the dining room. As they walked by the bar, Emilio went in to greet an uncle. He seemed to know the other men there. Tony waited outside and watched though the glass doors. He noticed how the men paid attention to him and how they all laughed when Emilio said something. Being his father's son had something to do with it. Everyone in Havana listened to the radio and heard his dad's jingles.

During the walk from the bar to the canopied entry area, where Emilio's chauffeur would be summoned on the loudspeakers set in the parking area, every boy they passed greeted Emilio. With other boys, Emilio was a celebrity. He was the main actor in many colorful stories that circulated at the Yacht Club.

Tony had a feeling that he and Emilio were going to be the main actors in one of those stories that afternoon. Tony liked how something interesting happened every time he had been with Emilio. In the process, he was starting to attach some interesting stories to his life. Up to now, not much had happened. He only hoped that the second episode in his sexual history would turn out to be more satisfying than the first one.

Roberto drove the impeccably clean and shiny white Mercedes under the canopy. Tony and Emilio climbed into the back seat.

"Where to?" Roberto asked, grinning.

"We'll go back to the Mambo next time," Emilio said, turning to Tony. "I want to try out another brothel today. I want to try them all! Roberto, take us to Marina."

Why not, Tony thought. Marina could not be much worse than

the Mambo. His cousin Ramiro claimed that he enjoyed going to Marina. Tony had some money with him this time, and one advantage about Marina was that it only cost three dollars.

MARINA was architecturally more interesting than the Mambo. The brothel occupied an old mansion close to the Malecón, the long seawall that protected Havana from the sea. The building had probably been built by a wealthy Spanish merchant during the colonial era and now was on its final legs in a colorful state of physical decay. The stucco walls had been painted over in various pastel colors over many decades of home improvements. Now the walls looked like colorful modern paintings: rain, sun and wind exposed the many paint layers at random. For the past few decades, home improvements had come to a halt.

The building had the typical floor plan of other buildings Tony had seen in Old Havana—all the rooms designed around a large open courtyard, paved with patterned blue and white Spanish tiles. Large potted plants at the edges of the courtyard created a lush tropical atmosphere, and in one corner of this jungle, in a large iron cage, a parrot reminded the customers why they were there, squawking endlessly in English: *Fuck the whores, fuck the whores.*

The parrot was clearly a tourist attraction. A group of American sailors drinking beer from the bottles stood around the parrot cage and laughed every time the parrot delivered his directives. Tony guessed that the closer a brothel got to the water, the more likely the clientele would be made up of tourists and sailors, although there were plenty of Cubans milling around. Everyone seemed to be staring at the women who sat in a row of wooden folding chairs set to one side of the courtyard.

A record player provided the music, and a few couples were

dancing. A small improvised bar served beer. Tony and Emilio ordered a couple of beers. Like the other men there, they sipped their beers and looked at the women.

Marina did not seem as classy as the Mambo. One of the women dancing kept lowering the top of her dress to show her breasts to her dancing partner. Tony knew that many boys from the Yacht Club came here, and he expected Ramiro and his gang of juvenile delinquents to appear at any moment. Ramiro did not show up, but they ran into someone else Tony knew: an older boy called Robertico Arteaga. Robertico was in the group ahead of them, the seventeen and eighteen-year-olds. He had dated Sofi, Tony's sister, a few times. Robertico had a reputation as a *ratón de bayú*, a brothel mouse, a reputation confirmed spectacularly that day. He was a basketball player for the Yacht Club, and a popular boy with the girls in Tony's sister's group. He was one of those boys who was utterly confident in his charm, his good looks, his persona and his scoring skills—both in and out of the court.

The moment he entered the courtyard, a few of the women started screaming: "Robertico! Robertico!" He seemed to have a fan club at Marina's. Tony was impressed. While it was not going to be his life goal, Tony knew that the chances of someone screaming "Tony! Tony!" when he entered a brothel was one in a trillion. Then a woman, who must have been Robertico's number one fan, heard the commotion in the courtyard and sprinted out of a room completely naked, leaving in her bed a very surprised customer. She ran down three flights of stairs, her long black hair flying wildly, all the while screaming "Robertico! Robertico!"

When she reached the courtyard she leaped into the air and threw herself at Robertico, arms and legs outstretched. Robertico caught her in mid air, effortlessly; as if fielding naked women was something he did frequently. Tony watched, stunned and impressed. Robertico had to be the world's greatest lover or simpatico beyond belief.

After that day, Tony paid attention every time Robertico visited his sister. He listened to what he said, watched his mannerisms, noticed his humor. He obviously knew something about pleasing women. The results were visible. Women left the ground and ignored gravity. They were drawn to him like a magnet.

Tony also figured that his sister had to eliminate him from her list of potential suitors. He thought his sister was very conventional, very religious, and he didn't expect her to be too interested in sex. Robertico, on the other hand, was a certified sexual maniac, another Gonzalo. It would not work out for them. For starters, there wasn't one chance in a million that Robertico would be faithful. If they married, Tony could envision how embarrassing it would be to run into his brother-in-law in a brothel.

Robertico, to his credit, was not about to disappoint his greatest fan. He walked up the stairs with her, his arm around her waist. Tony would have given anything to turn invisible, follow them into their room and watch them. He could learn a lot about what it took to be a great lover. In the meantime, Emilio was not wasting his time thinking about Robertico. He started dancing with the woman who had been exposing her breasts. He must have asked her if she could lower her top because she laughed out loud and lowered it. Emilio touched her breast, she slapped his hand, laughed and said something about going upstairs to do more of that. Emilio did not need further convincing, and they went up.

Emilio continued to impress Tony. He was all action. Tony admired him for it. Tony was the opposite. Tony was into inertia. If he was seated, his tendency was to remain seated. Before he did anything, his tendency was to think things over, analyze the options, the consequences. But he was trying to change.

He looked at the row of women seated against the wall. A

romantic Benny Moré song was playing on the record player. One thing Tony knew for sure—he was not going to find a romantic love with any of the women seated across the floor from him. That was what he wanted—to experience love, like the love that Benny Moré was singing about. For sure, it was not going to happen at Marina. It was more likely to happen with Carmen. In fact, it was already happening with Carmen.

It was embarrassing to be at Marina, even to look at the women. Some were trying to make eye contact with him, some were flashing smiles, but when he did not respond, they reverted to a look of profound disinterest. He did notice one girl. She seemed younger than the other women, and she was talking with the woman next to her, ignoring all the customers. She liked to talk, which was a good sign, and when she talked she became very animated. He had a good feeling about her. He was determined to choose someone interested in talking before doing it. She seemed like a good candidate.

He reminded himself about his project, about being a doer. He got up and walked across the courtyard until he stood in front of her. She ignored him at first. It was embarrassing. He stared at her, and she kept on talking to the woman next to her. Finally, she looked up. Tony blurted out: "Do you want to go up to a room with me?" She seemed surprised by his question. She looked at him and did not answer right away. Then she said: "Sure. Why not?" Tony dug into his pocket, gave her three dollars, and they walked up to a second floor bedroom.

They didn't talk on the way up, although she looked at him a few times and laughed, as if Tony's appearance amused her. The room she led him to was not as bare as the one at the Mambo. It looked lived in. He undressed quickly, piled all his clothes on a chair and then sat naked on the edge of the bed.

She seemed amused by his diligence. She started to undress, seemingly comfortable undressing in front of a stranger. She was thin and did not seem to have breasts, but she was pretty, with strangely short black hair and big eyes. She didn't wear makeup, like a normal girl. This is going to work out, Tony thought. He was clearly feeling attracted to her. He was determined, though, to have a conversation before they did anything. He wanted to get to know her and wanted her to know him, like normal people, before they had sex. While he waited for his partner to finish putting away her clothes, he became aware of voices coming from the room next to theirs.

The girl finished undressing and sat next to Tony on the edge of the bed, but she kept some distance between them. She stared at him curiously.

"How come you have blue eyes?"

Tony told her he had an Irish grandmother.

"How old are you?"

"Thirteen."

"I'm sixteen. My name is Alma."

"Hi. I'm Tony."

He was curious about how she had ended up in this room at Marina, but all he could come up with was:

"Do you go to school?"

She laughed. "No, I work here."

Tony thought of asking her why she was not going to school and living a normal life. Instead, he asked her:

"Do you like working here?"

She laughed again. "It's not great, but it's not too bad. I'm related to Marina. I can choose the men I go up with. I say no to most men who ask me to go upstairs. I'm very selective. I selected you. This is my permanent room."

"It's a nice room," Tony said. He liked the idea that he had been selected.

They stared at each other. It was awkward. Alma was not moving closer to him. He did not feel like initiating anything. But Alma kept smiling. She seemed to be enjoying the situation. He was feeling good about Alma. He was wondering how to keep the conversation going when he became aware of the voice of the woman in the room next to them. He could distinctly hear her pleading: "That's enough, that's enough, it hurts, please stop, stop…" and this refrain continued and continued. What was going on in there? It was disturbing. Alma was also listening.

"That one is a terrible client," she said. "I won't go in with him. That one, we know him here."

Tony was thinking about what Alma had just said. He couldn't imagine what the terrible client was doing with the girl next door.

"Are you a virgin?" Alma asked.

"No. I've done it once at the Mambo Club."

"Then you are almost a virgin," Alma said.

They stared at each other again. The voice pleading across the wall was getting louder. It was really bothersome. His mind was wondering from the business at hand. He liked Alma, but he noticed that he was no longer aroused. Alma noticed it too. She lay back on the bed and pulled him down. They rolled around a bit. The mattress' springs made surprisingly loud squeaks. The "stop, stop, stop," continued from the room next door.

He suddenly sat up in bed and asked her if they could stop for a minute. Did she mind if they talked for a while?

"I don't mind. I would much prefer to be paid just for conversation," Alma said, smiling.

"I'm nervous," Tony said.

"Relax," Alma said.

He looked around some more and noticed that Alma's room was fully furnished, like a regular room. Alma had left the closet open. He could see dresses hanging there. There was a chest of drawers against the wall with what looked like a family picture on top. A large stuffed bear sat in a chair by a small desk. Everything was very neat.

"You live here?" Tony asked.

"Yes. Want to see my music box?" Alma got up from the bed and went to the cabinet, opened a drawer and took out a small wooden music box. She came back to the bed, wound it up, opened the lid and held it on her hand. A small ballerina turned around while the box played a waltz.

"I bought it at El Tensen." That was the Cuban name for Woolworth, the Five and Ten-Cent Store. "Want to see my favorite dress?"

She left the music box on the bed and went back to the closet. She took out a plain blue cotton dress and held it against her body. The dress was patterned with naked baby angels.

"I like the angels," she said.

Tony agreed and said it was a nice dress. He asked her who was in the picture, looking toward the cabinet. Alma put her dress back in the closet and walked toward the picture. She lifted it up and looked at it. Then she put it down again.

"That's my family. I'm from Morón, in Camaguey."

She came back to the bed. Tony wondered about her family back in Morón and whether they knew the family situation in Havana.

She raised her knees up against her chest, picked up her music box, wound it again, put it on the bed and watched the ballerina turn and turn. She was really pleased with her music box. When it ran out, she wound up again. They both watched the ballerina, and listened to the music, which mingled with the murmurs from the room next door: The woman was now pleading: "That's enough, that's enough, that's enough."

"So," Alma said, "Do you want to do it?"

Tony liked Alma, but he did not feel like going through with it. The goings-on next door were very bothersome. At that moment, he felt sorry for the girl next door and felt sorry for Alma and how she lived alone in this room with her angel dresses, and how she seemed to treasure her inexpensive music box and how Marina was her evil stepmother. Doing it with Alma did not feel right.

"Actually, I'm not in the mood right now. I hope you don't mind. Let's go downstairs, but don't tell anyone that we didn't do it." He did not plan to tell Emilio.

"Don't worry," she said. "I think you're too young for this." She started to get dressed.

The woman next door was still protesting while he quickly dressed. He could not get out of that room fast enough.

THE following day after school, he went with Gonzalo on an errand to Old Havana. The streets, as usual, were jammed. Tony was seated up front with Gonzalo, looking out the window, noticing how there was at least one bar in every block of Old Havana. The traffic stalled the car opposite a bar. He could see inside and noticed a woman, dressed provocatively, sitting alone at the bar, nursing a drink, possibly waiting for some man to sit next to her. The opportunities to buy sex in Havana were endless. He was learning, though, that sex that was paid for was not that satisfying. Not for him, and not for that woman in the room next to his at Marina's. He felt sorry for Alma. She seemed so fragile. He asked Gonzalo why some women were prostitutes.

"I could not tell you why. It's complicated," Gonzalo said. "But

I can tell you it's a good thing they do. It's necessary for society. Without prostitution, many marriages would not last. With prostitution, there is less divorce. They say that prostitution was the first profession. That tells you something. It's necessary for society to function."

"But it's not so good if you are the prostitute," Tony said. "They have to put up with all sorts of perverts. Why would anyone want that job?"

"You're not too smart, are you? For the money! There aren't that many jobs for women, and most jobs for women require skills; they need shorthand or typing skills. You don't need a skill to become a prostitute. Some people say that prostitution is a disgrace, a symptom of a sick society and a symptom of poverty. That is probably true. I think the problems of Cuba are caused by corruption, by greedy politicians. The communists, on the other hand, say that all the prostitution in Havana is the fault of the Americans."

"How could it be the fault of the Americans?"

"Because when American sailors or tourists come to Cuba, the first thing they want to do is go to a brothel."

"Gonzalo, you're not a communist, are you?"

"Are you kidding? Communists are fools, and your grandfather would fire me if I were a communist. Politics don't interest me. The last time I was interested in politics was when Chibás was around, and look what he did."

Everyone in Cuba, even Tony, remembered Eduardo "Eddy" Chibás. In the early fifties, the kitchen radio was always turned on during his weekly radio show—dedicated to denouncing the corruption of Cuban politicians. His family didn't care for him, but the servants loved him. Then Chibás decided that the system was so hopelessly corrupt that it could not be changed. As an act of protest, he shot himself during his weekly radio show. Everyone in Cuba was horrified. Some said afterward that it was a public-ity stunt. That he had only intended to wound himself, but he missed and died. In any case, no new political heroes emerged in the kitchen.

There had been some talk about Fidel Castro, an ex-student leader from the University of Havana, who had tried to start a revolt against Batista the previous summer. Castro and a group of his followers attacked an army barrack in Oriente province, but the attack was a disaster and almost everyone was killed. Castro miraculously survived because the soldier who found him in a cane field had orders to kill him, but didn't. Castro ended up in jail. Now no one talked about him.

The traffic had stalled them again, and he could see into an-other bar. There was a jukebox in there playing a Rolando LaSerie song. A couple was dancing next to the jukebox. Tony could tell by their body language, how they clung to each other, that those two were in love. No money was involved in that union. That was what he wanted.

ON his last day of class at Belén, after five years there, he was surprised that he did not feel any sadness when he walked out the door for the last time. He was not leaving many close friends behind. He did not know why that was so. He didn't play any team sports. That was one reason. Also, he was aware that there was a class difference between him and most students. Most students at Belén came from the middle class. They lived in average size houses or in one of those new apartment buildings that were going up all over the city, and maybe they had a maid or two. He did not think that he was a snob, but very few of his classmates belonged to the Yacht Club or the Country Club or had summer homes on Varadero Beach. So on weekends and during summer vacations, he never saw any of them.

The Jesuits weren't all bad. He was going to miss some of them. He was especially going to miss having confession with Father Zulueta. He had not confessed his brothel activities, but he was sure that Father Zulueta would have understood. Try to be better, he would have advised. Watch out for venereal diseases, he might have added.

Tony was not going to miss some of his teachers. He still remembered Brother Ignacio, his fourth grade Sacred History teacher, who did not allow students to go to the bathroom during his class. One day, in his class, he needed to pee badly. He had been holding it through a few other classes, and then he had to go. He raised his hand and asked for permission to go to the bathroom. Brother Ignacio said no. Instead, he asked Tony to get up in front of the class and read from the sacred history book. Maybe he thought that reading sacred history would overcome his need to pee, but halfway through the reading he could not hold it any longer. He brought the book very close to his face and stopped reading. The pee stained his Khaki pants, then trickled down his leg and formed a puddle on the raised wooden platform.

The class was shocked. They were dead silent at first, and then they started laughing, somewhat nervously, then raucously. Tony stood there, frozen, the book now firmly pressed against his face. That was his worst memory of Belén. Not many things could be worse than peeing in your pants in front of your classmates.

On the bus trip home, he felt happy. This was the best moment of the year—the last bus ride from school and the beginning of summer vacation. Within a week, he would be swimming in the clear waters of Varadero Beach. The only thought that dampened his mood was that Emilio was picking him up that evening, and they were going to the Mambo Club.

Going to the Mambo had him worried. He had thought more than a few times about Alma since Sunday. He liked her, but he had been incapable of having sex with her. With Sylvia, he had sex so fast that he had established a new world record. He had been attending the Havana Sex Academy, and he was flunking out. Emilio, of course, was getting straight As, loving every moment of it and doing it twice every time. Tony would not be surprised if that night, on entering the Mambo, a woman jumped into Emilio's arms, yelling, "Emilio! Emilio!"

12

NO ONE PAID MUCH ATTENTION
when they walked in. Now that they were Mambo Club veter-
ans, they tried not to look too wide-eyed. They sat down at the
same table near the dance floor, ordered rum and cokes and
looked around. Tony noticed right away that Sylvia was dancing
with another boy—another victim—and she was working him over
with her pelvic grind and her sweet talk. He should warn that boy
that he was going to experience lighting fast sex followed by the
thought: What! Is that it?

He had to admit, though, that Sylvia was smart. By concentrating on young boys, she avoided the demanding, perverted clients,
like the bad customer in the room next to his at Marina. And the
fast turnovers could net Sylvia a lot of money in one evening. If it
was all about money, as Gonzalo claimed, she might as well make

her business efficient and painless. He couldn't blame her for that, but he was not going in with her again.

Emilio snapped his fingers and yelled *garçon* at one of the waiters. Emilio called waitresses *"mi amor"* and waiters *"garçon"* and said other embarrassing things, but no one seemed to mind because he tipped them well. Emilio told Tony that he learned to tip from his father. During their European trips, the Eloys were treated like royalty when they arrived at hotels. The staff remembered the extravagant tips from the previous summer. Emilio had barely started sipping his drink before he was up and dancing. He had mentioned on the ride over that he was going to feel up as many women as possible on the dance floor before going in with someone. Tony had to admit that dancing the cha-cha-chá at the Mambo Club was a special treat.

While sipping his drink, Tony wondered what disaster awaited him this time. He looked around. There was a woman sitting two tables away from him. She was dressed in black, which matched her dark hair well. Most of the women sat in groups, in larger tables, but this one sat in a small, just-for-two table. She was smoking a cigarette, blowing perfect smoke rings toward the ceiling, concentrating on making them come out exactly right. She was good at it. She must have sensed that Tony was watching because she turned her face toward him. She did not smile, or make any effort to please him; she simply stared at him. If she was soliciting him, she was subtle about it. She probably knew that her not smiling was very effective, the way models in his mother's *Vogue Magazine* never smiled. She knew that she did not need to do much to get men interested in her. After staring at Tony for a few seconds, she went back to blowing her perfect smoke rings toward the ceiling.

Tony took two long gulps of his Cuba Libre. He liked this woman. He looked at her again and thought that she was older, maybe close to thirty. She reminded him of his mother's friend, Sylvia Machado, who was painfully attractive and mysterious. Although she was sitting down, he could tell she had a nice figure. Her dress revealed enough of her chest to interest any man in seeing more.

He had to ask this Sylvia Machado to dance. His new strategy at the Mambo called for him doing the choosing. Dancing with her would be exciting, especially if she was adept at the pelvic grind. But he was nervous. He felt glued to his chair. He thought again about Mr. Eloy and the *Charge of the Light Brigade*; into the jaws of death, into the mouth of hell, rode the six hundred. Do it, he ordered himself. He gulped down the last of his Cuba Libre and stood up.

He walked over, rehearsing some opening lines: "Hello, how are you?"; "Hello, let's dance"; "Hello, let's dance and then let's make love"; "Hello, you remind me of my mother's most beautiful friend". What would Cary Grant say in a movie?: "Madam, may I?" as he sat down. Or: "Madam, I have a weakness for beautiful women who blow perfect smoke rings."

As he approached her table, she said: "I was wondering when you were going to come over."

"Really!" Tony was impressed.

"Shall we go in?"

"Sure."

"Okay."

And they went in. The new room did not have a mirror over the bed, which was a good thing. He did not care for that detail. If the mirror fell, it could kill him. He would forever be known in de la Torre family lore as the boy who was killed by a falling mirror in a brothel. Women in his family would whisper the story and conclude with: it was an act of God.

As soon as she entered the room, she started to slip off her dress. Tony was standing in the middle of the room, making no moves.

"Are you planning to have sex with your clothes on?" She asked, amused.

"No," Tony said. "But would you mind if we talk a little before we do it? I don't even know your name."

"Isabel, that's my name," she said. "Honey, if you take off our clothes and get in bed, I might even tell you my middle name."

"Okay," Tony said.

He sat on a chair next to the closet and took off his shoes and his socks. He stood up, took off his shirt, hung it on a hanger, then took off his pants and hung them, too. He kept on his shorts. He turned around and saw that Isabel was sitting at the edge of the bed, completely naked. She gestured for him to come to her. Tony moved closer and stood in front of her. Isabel extended her arms and lowered his boxer shorts, revealing his erect penis. She patted the bed next to her. Tony sat down. The mattress was not firm, and they sank in together. She turned off the light next to the bed. The room had one window with long wooden shutters, and the shutters were partially open. Light from a street light outside seeped into the room and projected long stripes of light on their bodies. He could hear the crickets outside, some frogs and some dogs barking. Her breasts were perfectly proportioned. He stared at them.

"You want to touch them?" Isabel said, amused.

"Sure." He raised his hand and touched the tip of her breast. Then, very lightly, he touched the whole breast.

"Do you like them?"

"Sure. I like them a lot."

"You can touch them with both hands, if you like."

"Okay." He touched them with both hands.

"Do you want to lick them?"

This request took him by surprise. Licking breasts had never been featured in any of his fantasies.

"No, thank you."

"Don't be silly! Go ahead!"

"No, it's not necessary," Tony said.

"Honey, nothing we do here is necessary. Here, let's get more comfortable." She lay back on the bed.

"Come here, honey. Let's kiss."

That request surprised him too. So far, he had not kissed anyone in a brothel. In fact, he had not kissed anyone outside a brothel. This proposal interested him. Tony moved up to her, and they kissed, lying on their sides. She pulled back.

"That's too quick, honey. You want to linger. Like this."

She moved her mouth close to Tony and then closer. She played with his lips, sucking them gently, like a lollipop. That was interesting, Tony thought. Then he felt her tongue trying to get into his mouth. That was not so interesting. He moved his face back.

Isabel laughed. "What's your name?"

"Tony."

"Well, Tony, you want to do it?"

"Sure."

He was erect, but did not know exactly how to steer his penis into her. She helped him. Isabel was straddling him, still on her side, and she started moving to a slow, languid beat. She was in no rush to get it over with. Her hands were holding tight to the back of his thighs, and she was pressing him in and out.

It felt good. Their two bodies were moving in unison. He didn't want this activity to end too quickly. Okay, he thought: Gonzales bats first and plays second base; Roberto Ortiz, center field, bats second; although he was a power hitter, better have him bat fourth.

But Tony's attempt to think of a baseball lineup was hopeless. He felt his orgasm coming on like an onrushing train, and there was no stopping it.

"Ay hijo! That happens," she said. "Let's wait fifteen minutes, which is all it will take for you to recharge. I would like you to be one of my regular clients."

"Sure," Tony said. He would not mind doing it regularly with Isabel. He could do it every day if she wanted to.

They sat up in bed, leaning against the backboard of the bed. Isabel had pulled up the white sheet over her breasts, an unexpected act of modesty.

"You have many regular clients? I bet you do."

"Yes, I do. You were lucky that I had an opening. I usually only go in with my regulars, but you seemed like a nice boy."

"Do you like this job? You do it very well."

"*Mi amor*," she said, laughing. "That is very sweet of you. You are very amusing. So you think I do it very well. That's nice. A lot of my clients agree. One of my regulars wants to set me up in an apartment in one of those tall buildings by the Malecón with a view of the sea. I think he's serious. He wants me to leave this job. He wants me all for himself. He's very jealous."

Tony could see why someone might feel that way.

"He's married, but I don't mind. I like him. He would visit a few times a week. In the meantime, I would like to go to school and learn shorthand, learn English. To get ahead nowadays, one has to learn English. Do you know English?" And without waiting for his answer she asked him: "You want to kiss some more?"

"Sure."

She uncovered herself, and they reclined on the bed, in a side-by-side position. Isabel started playing with his mouth again. They kissed for a while, and then she said: "I think you are ready for another go."

She was right. She guided him in, wrapped herself around Tony, and pressed him in and out like a rubber doll. He was really enjoying having sex with Isabel. And she was right. He didn't come right away, and he didn't even have to think of the baseball line-up.

TONY went back to their table. Emilio was not on the dance floor so he had probably found someone he liked and was in a bedroom. Tony felt like celebrating and ordered another Cuba Libre. He had finally passed sex class. He truly had enjoyed doing it with Isabel, and he was certain that she had enjoyed it too. Now he was starting to understand why everyone made such a big deal about sex. He could envision becoming one of Isabel's regulars, although he was running out of time and out of money. His savings came from Christmas, Saint's days and birthdays, and he had not saved that much. He had enough for three more times. Emilio had talked about coming back to the Mambo on Saturday and maybe Sunday, and he might get Gonzalo to bring him one more time before he left for Varadero Beach.

He thought about what Isabel had told him about her jealous lover and the apartment he was going to get her. If it was he, and he had the money, he would do it. He would set her up in a nice apartment and visit her often. More than twice a week. He could pass by her apartment every day, have lunch there on a balcony with the view of the ocean, make love to Isabel after lunch, then go back to the office. That routine would make going to work every day something to look forward to.

He looked around again and saw that Isabel was making her way back to her table. Tony watched her and could not help admiring how well she carried herself. He did not doubt what she had said about having a dedicated and regular clientele. How long was that list, he wondered. How many men did she do it with in one day? Did she like them as much as she seemed to like him?

The moment Isabel sat down, a man came up to her table. After a brief conversation, they walked together to the back of the club. He was undoubtedly one of her regulars because they were talking and laughing, like old friends. For the first time in his life, Tony felt jealous. That man was making her laugh more than he had.

THE next day, after school, Tony went out on an errand with Gonzalo. He told him about Isabel, and how much he had enjoyed doing it with her. He also told him about her apartment plans and asked if Gonzalo's thought he would have to pay her if she got the apartment.

Gonzalo laughed. "Yes, and not only will you have to pay her, but now you'll have to pay twice or three times as much because she'll have more overhead."

"But her boyfriend is going to be paying the rent."

"Tony, don't be such an idiot. Look, here are the rules. You go to a brothel, you pay your money, you do it and you get on with your life. That's it. If you want a lasting relationship, you do that with a decent girl. You have it backwards."

Gonzalo always made sense, but this time he did not understand the situation. He had not been in the room with Isabel. He did not know her. She was different.

NOW it was Tony who could not wait to go back to the Mambo, and Emilio was the one who seemed to feel lukewarm about going back on Saturday. They had talked on the telephone, and Emilio mentioned that there was a good movie playing at the Rodi. Something must have happened the last time at the Mambo, although he had not said a thing. Tony insisted on going back. He told Emilio he wanted to go in with Isabel again and how this weekend was his last chance to do it with her before moving to Varadero.

"Okay. Let's go on Saturday," Emilio said. "But there is something we need to talk about when you come for lunch."

ON Saturday, on the way to Emilio's house, Gonzalo pulled a stunt unlike any Tony had ever seen before. They were driving westward in Miramar, on Fifth Avenue. Gonzalo approached a woman walking on the right sidewalk. Tony could tell that she had the kind of figure that called for a serious slowdown or a complete halt. Gonzalo slowed the car down, watched her as they passed, then continued driving for half a block, parked the car and got out. He said: "Watch this!"

He walked back to meet her, and just before they intersected, Gonzalo quickly took off his gray jacket and used it as an improvised broom to dust the sidewalk in the woman's path. Tony watched as they passed by him. Gonzalo walked backward in front of the woman, bent down and frantically dusted away. He did it for almost a full block, and she did not even seem to break her stride. But clearly, she was amused. Gonzalo finally stopped and said something to her as she passed him by. She smiled, but continued walking. Gonzalo stood there and continued saying things to her, but she never looked back. Gonzalo dusted his jacket against his pants, put it on again and returned to the car.

"I think I pulled my back," he said. "And my jacket is a mess, and she did not give me her phone number. But did you see how pleased she looked?"

THEY were sitting in Emilio's room. Emilio was showing him an album of photographs from his last European trip, and the Leica camera that he had used to take the pictures. The camera intrigued

Tony. He had a Kodak Brownie, a little plastic box, which took good pictures, but this camera was an expensive 35-mm camera, and the pictures Emilio showed him were razor sharp.

Tony got interested in taking pictures when his parents sent him to Camp Pasquaney in New Hampshire, and they had bought him the Brownie. Every Sunday, there was a quiet period after lunch when the campers had to write letters to their parents. Tony sent pictures—views from the top of the mountain that his hiking group had climbed that week. He took four shots; north, east, south, west, and every Sunday he sent the drugstore prints home. The letters said: Hi Mom, here is the mountain I climbed this week. I'm having lots of fun. Love, Tony.

Now Emilio was talking about what he had mentioned on the phone. He had told his father about their trips to the Mambo. He figured his father would not mind because he had already told him that he would not stand in his way. But Mr. Eloy was upset.

"Guess what he was upset about," he asked Tony.

"Because we're too young," Tony ventured.

"Yes and no. He thinks we are too young, but that is not why he's so upset. Guess again."

"I don't know. Because we lied about going to the movies, and Bernard Baruch would have never done that."

"No, guess again."

"I give up."

"Because we didn't wear condoms! We can't go again unless we wear condoms. Here, I've already bought them." Emilio dug into a paper bag sitting on his desk and pulled out a handful of individually wrapped condoms. He opened one up and showed it to Tony.

"They are tricky to put on. I've been experimenting. You have to have an erection, and then you roll them on. I'll show you. He left the room and came back shortly. He had taken a short, stubby Partagas from his father's cigar box. He sat down and carefully rolled the condom onto the cigar. "See, it's easy," he said, passing the condomized cigar to Tony.

At lunch, Tony could tell that Mr. Eloy was in a bad mood. No stories about Bernard Baruch or other great men. No advice of any kind. No stories about his past. Tony guessed that he was unusually quiet because he knew what they were doing after lunch. He must have sensed that he could control most things, including an army of workers that marched to his orders, but boys growing up in Havana were going to do what boys in Havana always did—they went to brothels. Still, it was obvious that Mr. Eloy was not happy about it. It was an unusually quiet lunch. After lunch, Emilio's mother asked him where they were going, and Emilio offered the standard lie—to the movies—and they were gone.

ISABEL was not on the floor when they sat down at their regular table, so Tony assumed that she was busy with one of her regulars. They ordered drinks and were sipping their Cuba Libres when he saw Isabel making her way back to her small table.

Tony sprang into action. He got up and intercepted her before she even sat down.

"Como estás, mi amor," she said.

"I'm well. Can I go in with you again?"

"Oh, how sweet," she said, smiling. "Honey, I have some regulars waiting at the bar. There is a line today, but I'll put you in line. I think there are two in front of you. Maybe three. But wait."

Third in line! His face must have reflected his disappointment.

"Sure, I'll wait, but I'm here with my friend, and he might not want to wait too long. We have to go back home."

"I'll tell you what I'll do because you are so sweet. I'll take my next customer, and then I'll slip you in after that. How's that?" She smiled.

"That's better. Thanks."

And almost on cue, a handsome middle-aged man wearing an expensive linen *guayabera* approached them. Isabel moved toward him and greeted him with a loud "Carlos!" She seemed genuinely delighted to see him. He did not seem to be the one that was next in line because she seemed surprised. They hugged. He whispered something to her. She broke out laughing. Carlos smiled at Tony, put his arm around Isabel's waist, and they made their way to the back door. Tony could hear Isabel laughing again and again as they disappeared through the door. Carlos must have been a comedian.

Tony sat down at his table, feeling miserable. Emilio, Captain Action, was already dancing. Tony wondered if Carlos was the mystery man, the man who wanted to set up Isabel in an apartment. He could not help notice how Isabel had seemed so happy to see him, how she had laughed so heartily at everything he said. And Carlos was older, attractive and looked well off. He was a man of the world, very self-assured and probably had all sorts of interesting and sophisticated adult things to say. Tony knew he could not compete with Carlos. Carlos was in another league.

He had plenty of time to speculate about Carlos because Isabel was gone for a long time. In addition to being good looking and suave and rich, Carlos was very likely a terrific lover. Emilio was doing his best to follow in Carlos' footsteps. He had gone in and had returned, and now was dancing again with another woman. Tony had explained to Emilio his predicament, and how he had to wait.

"Don't worry," Emilio said. "I don't mind waiting. I'll go in again. It will be a new record: four times!"

Tony had positioned his chair so he could keep an eye on the back door. He was watching when Isabel and Carlos returned. Carlos was a classy guy. He held both her hands, kissed her on her mouth and then went to the bar. Isabel was making her way back to her table. Tony got up quickly and intercepted her.

"Isabel, I'm still here, waiting," he said.

"Yes, I can see that," she said. "I'll do you a favor. Let's go."

TONY'S second time with Isabel was a disaster. First of all, Isabel seemed distracted. She wasn't focused on him. She was thinking about something else, possibly thinking about Carlos, because she didn't want to talk much like during their first time. Maybe Carlos had changed his mind about the apartment. He might have looked into it and found that the rents were too high for apartments with an ocean view. In any case, Isabel didn't look too happy, and she didn't offer to kiss him on the mouth.

What was more bothersome was that she seemed to want to get it over with very fast. Then there was the condom. It was difficult to put it on, and when he finally managed, it felt weird, and he instantly lost his erection. Isabel appeared impatient. He got rid of the condom. When they finally did it, Isabel didn't offer to do it a second time. She said she had a long line of customers waiting at the bar, and she had to move on, so she had him out of her room fast. The second time with Isabel reminded him of his first time at the Mambo.

On the ride home, Tony was silent. Emilio was not saying much either. He said he had done it three times and tried to do it a fourth, but couldn't. Tony was thankful that Emilio was not talking much and was not telling him how much he had enjoyed doing it three times.

He was trying to understand what had happened. Isabel had

been so nice the first time, and this time she wasn't nice at all. Almost every outing to a brothel had been a minor disaster, and this last one had to be classified as a major disaster because he had been looking forward so much to doing it again with her.

Someone like Robertico Arteaga, and even Emilio, might thrive at the brothels, but it was not working for him. Having sex with a stranger, for pay, at his age, was too complicated. It was not normal, and it was not fun. The solution to the problem was obvious; he would stop going to brothels. He had done it, gone through the age-old Havana ritual, and now it was time to move on. Maybe he might go back to the brothels when he was older, when he was Carlos' age, and he no longer enjoyed having sex with his wife. But right now, he was dreading the thought of another bad episode at the Mambo or at Marina. What he wanted was to experience love with a normal girl.

His first problem: what to tell Emilio. He did not want to come across as cowardly or not manly. Still, he should be honest and tell him exactly what he was thinking. He was also getting tired of going along with everything that Emilio proposed. Roberto dropped him off by the gates to his house, and Tony decided not to go in just yet. He crossed the street and walked onto the median strip. G Street was one of the finest avenues in Havana, with the up and down sides separated by an attractive landscaped park that ran the entire length of the avenue. A broad concrete walkway ran down the center with park benches on both sides. During the day, nannies and children populated the park. The nannies sat together on the benches and talked, while the children under their care roller-skated or rode bicycles. At night, lovers took over the benches.

Tony walked for half a block before he found an empty bench and sat down. Two couples were seated on the benches facing his. One couple stared straight ahead and barely talked. Maybe they had a fight, or were changing their mind about getting married, or were married, and now they were thinking that they had made a terrible mistake.

The other couple stared lovingly into each other's eyes and held hands. Occasionally one or the other said something, and the other laughed. That pair was in love. They were certain that they were made for each other, and they were equally certain that their love would last forever. They had fallen head-over-heels in love.

That was what Tony wanted. He wanted to experience a romantic love and all the feelings that went along with it. He wanted to feel like that couple and like the singers who sang the love songs on the radio. That head-over-heels couple would get married. When they had sex, that sexual union surely would be an extraordinary experience. That was the Cuban sequence: you liked a person, you fell in love, you carried out an extended courtship without touching or kissing, you became intensely sexually aroused, you married, you had sex and because of all that waiting, the sexual experience had to be fantastic. He had started the sequence backwards—from the end, with no feelings at all. At the brothels, there was just sex, and sex was not enough. He had to start the sequence where one was supposed to start it—with head-over-heels falling in love.

13

WHEN HE WOKE UP ON SUNDAY morning, he felt relieved. During the previous night he had a rare moment of revelation and resolve, but now he had to tell Emilio. He still wanted to be his friend, but they had to come up with something else to do. They could go to the movies as they had been claiming all along, or go visit the Cuban girls in their group or visit the American girls Emilio claimed he knew. They could do anything that Sunday except what they had planned: going to the Mambo Club after lunch.

He was sitting alone at the children's table in the pantry, having a breakfast of *café con leche* and Cuban bread. He was thinking about how was he going to explain his revelation to Emilio without offending the Eloy's Charge of the Light Brigade attitude toward life. He heard the phone ring. A moment later the butler came into the pantry and told him that Emilio Eloy was on the telephone.

Tony walked to the living room and sat by the small telephone desk next to the main staircase. He noticed that there was a new copy of the Social Guide next to the telephone. It was edited by Joaquín de Posada, the man who wrote the social pages section in the Diario de la Marina, the best Havana newspaper. Every year he included a few more families in the Guide. Tony had heard that for new families to get in, they had to pay him a lot of money. He picked up the telephone. He still didn't know what he was going to say.

"Tony, you won't believe what's happened," Emilio said. He could not imagine what was coming, but he was learning to be cautious about Emilio's surprises.

"What?"

"Take a wild guess. It has something to do with the brothels."

"They've been outlawed!"

"No. I got crabs!"

"What?"

"I got crabs. You might have them, too."

"How can you tell you have crabs?"

"It itches down there. I looked at my pubic hair with a magnifying glass, and I saw them. Do you itch at all?"

Now he was alarmed. He thought: yes, he had felt some itching down there that morning. He had assumed it was an irritation caused by the condom.

"I felt something."

"I bet you have them, too," Emilio said. "Everyone who goes to brothels gets them. It's not a big deal. Come to my house for lunch. I have a microscope, and we can examine them. Don't worry. Drug stores are closed today, but on Monday morning we'll go to Drogeria Sarrá in Old Havana, and we'll buy some good anti-crab shampoo."

IN Emilio's room they sat at the edge of his bed, pants down and took turns inspecting their pubic hair with a magnifying glass. Emilio showed Tony some of his crabs; a few tiny black critters hunkered down at the base of his pubic hair. Tony took the magnifying glass and looked for them in his pubic hair. He quickly found a few.

Emilio set up his science kit microscope. With a pair of tweezers he yanked one of his pubic hairs out. It had a crab wrapped around it and he carefully placed it under the microscope. They took turns looking at it. The crab, magnified, was impressive—a ferocious looking monster, like a creature from another planet. It was scary, and it was sucking their blood.

Thankfully, Emilio didn't say anything about going again to the Mambo. That Sunday they went to the John Wayne movie playing at the Rodi.

ON Monday morning, Emilio's chauffeur took them to the Sarrá drugstore on Obispo Street. Drogeria Sarrá was the largest and one of the oldest drugstores in Havana. It was an elegant establishment with beautifully crafted wooden shelves and a long marble counter. It belonged to a family Tony knew from Varadero Beach, but he knew that no family members worked there.

Emilio, not embarrassed at all, told the young female attendant at the counter that he wanted to buy two very large bottles of their strongest anti-crab shampoo. She laughed, seemingly amused by Emilio's request. She walked to a shelf on the back wall and came back carrying two large dark glass bottles and a heavy brown paper to put them in. She put the bottles in the bag, still smiling. Emilio paid her. Tony grabbed the bag, and they walked out.

Emilio suggested they walk the few blocks to El Encanto. He needed to buy new sunglasses.

When they got to the store, they went up the steps that led to the side entrance. Then something amazing happened. During his recent ordeal at the brothels, he had almost forgotten about Carmen Macía. As they opened the door to go in, they nearly crashed into Carmen and Tina, who were going out. Tony immediately thought: what were the odds for something like that happening? It had to be a sign.

They stayed outside and talked briefly because the girls were late for their next appointment—they were meeting Tía Nina for lunch at the Floridita. They were loaded with shopping bags—getting ready for the beach season on Varadero Beach. As they talked, Tony was thinking that Carmen seemed focused on him. This was the girl he wanted.

His next project was to fall in love with a normal girl his age, a girl like Carmen. Shortly after that thought, he caught Carmen looking at his brown paper bag. Tony knew it would be a matter of seconds before Carmen asked him about its contents. What a disaster! His plan to connect with Carmen someday, and have an idyllic future together, could suffer a catastrophic setback if Carmen discovered that his brown paper bag contained two gigantic anti-crab shampoo bottles.

"Tony de la Torre," Carmen said, with a mischievous tone. "What is in that bag? Whatever you have there, you didn't buy it in a very elegant store."

"Yes, we went to the outdoor market and bought some mangos for the cook."

"What a lie!" Carmen said quickly. "You don't have mangos in there. When we nearly crashed at the door I heard a clicking sound."

Tony had to think fast. What he said next could affect his future.

"Okay, I won't lie. We bought two bottles of rum, but it's not for us. It's for Roberto, Emilio's chauffeur. It's his birthday."

"He's forty-two today," Emilio said.

"If it's really for the chauffeur, that's nice," Carmen said, satisfied.

They said their goodbyes, and they were gone.

Roberto dropped Tony at his house. Emilio gave him the brown bag with one of the bottles. When he got in the house, he went straight to his bathroom, took a shower and applied the shampoo. After a few days of two-a-day shampoos, dead crabs collected on his shorts.

14

THE FIRST WEEK ON VARADERO
Beach was a welcome change-of-pace for Tony. He badly needed
a vacation from Havana, Emilio and the brothels. Tony was still
reminded of his disastrous attempt at the profligate life every time
he found another dead crab in the lining of his bathing suit. He
liked Emilio, but he wished he had not met him. His life was duller
before he met Emilio, but now he yearned for some dullness in
his life. He looked forward to being independent again. He looked
forward to his beach routine—a calm, low-key routine.

On Varadero, the crabs he normally encountered made him
smile. Tony's house faced a fine white sand beach that was home
to an army of small sand colored ghost crabs, scurrying over the
sand with their super quick six legs and their tiny periscope eyes.
Varadero Beach was all about nature, about observing it and being

amazed by it. Mostly, it was about living very close to the water. He never got tired of watching the ocean from his porch and how it had a different appearance every day. Varadero reminded him that he lived on a tropical island. In Havana, one could easily forget that.

He loved the sounds of the beach. At night, when he went to sleep in his room, he could only hear the soothing sounds of the palm fronds right outside his window and the rhythmic crashing and receding of the waves. His room was always breezy; there was no need for air conditioning. If he stepped outside, he could see an explosion of stars. In Havana, the city lights made it hard to see them. Here, he could see every visible star in the Milky Way. He could smell the salt in the air and taste it when he licked his forearm.

Cocó built his summer home as close to the water as possible. A low concrete wall separated the front lawn from the sand and kept the sea at bay during storms. The architect who designed Cocó's house had a preference for white stucco walls, red Spanish tile roofs with generous overhangs and wide tiled porches. Glass doors opened the living and dining areas to the porches and beyond the porches to the ocean.

A bedroom wing with eight bedrooms on an upper level jutted at an angle to the back of the property, with views of an inland lagoon on the corridor side and views of the ocean on the other side. The eight bedrooms were fully occupied during the summer. In addition to the Havana household, Cocó's third daughter joined them, along with her husband and another set of cousins who were all younger than Tony. The only Campos offspring missing was Cocó's only son, Tina's dad, who had his own house on the beach.

The day after he arrived, Tony woke up at dawn, leaped out of bed and walked to the porch to look at the ocean. It was as calm as a lake, and this usually meant it was a good day for fishing. The ocean in front of his house had a clear sand bottom. This early in the morning, before the bathers and the motorboats scared them off, he could usually spot large fish—barracudas and small sharks—hunting for sardines close to the surf. He scanned the beachfront for large moving shadows but saw nothing. He went to the kitchen and started a pot of coffee, then went down the outside stairs behind the kitchen to the servants' rooms on the ground floor to make sure Ramón, the resident fisherman, was up.

Ramón grew up in Camarioca, the fishing village not far from Varadero. Like everyone else in that village, Ramón knew how to fish, and he knew the ocean. He could find the best spots for bottom fishing and could tell, to the minute, when they had to pull anchor and turn back because a bad squall was coming. During the winter, he took care of Cocó's house and fished for himself. During the summer, in addition to keeping up with the garden, he took care of the boat and drove it when the family water-skied. Almost every morning, he fished for the house with Tony.

The current boat, an eighteen-foot Correct Craft with a powerful inboard, was anchored in front of the house. It could pull four skiers at the same time, and Tony's mother, aunts and all the children skied. But skiing never got going until late in the morning, after Tony and Ramón came back from fishing. With the Correct Craft they could go out further and get there faster than with their previous boats, and they caught bigger fish—the large snappers and groupers which Rolando cooked in his delicious green sauce.

After a quick breakfast of Cuban bread and coffee, Tony and Ramón carried the lines and the bait to the boat, then drove at top speed straight out from the house. After a few miles, they slowed down. The water was as clear as glass, and they could see the patterns on the bottom, thirty or forty meters below. Finding good spots for fishing was a science. They had markers on land they lined up to locate the exact spot that had been good to them in the past: a palm tree with the radio tower on the left, the tip of a hill and another palm tree on the right. They dropped anchor, lowered their lines and waited.

Tony and Ramón did not talk much. They looked at the ocean, listened to the sounds of the water lapping the boat, focused on their lines and let their minds wander. Tony was thinking about how hectic and strange his life had been in Havana during the past few weeks, but now he sensed how calm and relaxing it felt to be here, floating on the ocean.

Then he felt the first bites. Those were tiny nibbles, and he knew he had some three and four-inch fish picking at his bait. Then he felt a more substantial bite. That was a much bigger fish. He became very focused and waited for just the right moment. When he felt the bite again, he yanked the line hard, hooked the fish and then started pulling up the nylon line by hand.

He could tell from the pull that it was a big fish, but the excitement of ocean fishing was that he never knew exactly what was on the line until the fish was visible, ten meters under, still fighting hard to stay in his world. He pulled the fish out, a large red snapper, unhooked him and threw the fish in one of the buckets. He always felt sorry for the fish when he watched it die, eyes wide open, frantically gasping for oxygen. But his sorrow for the fish never lasted long; he re-baited quickly and dropped the line again. Tony knew they would eat that snapper that afternoon at lunch. It was a good feeling, a primal feeling—to catch the food the family ate. It made killing the fish acceptable, and Cocó would be pleased.

Cocó had been generous about buying boats the moment he

realized he never again had to buy fish during the summer months to feed his large household. He first bought a boat for the grand-children when Tony was six. It was nine-feet long, and it had a two-horsepower outboard—too small a boat for the ocean, but perfect for the lagoon. The lagoon was a breeding ground for bar-racudas. The only fish they caught there were baby barracudas, but Cubans don't eat barracudas. What barracudas feed on causes serious indigestion.

The next boat was a twelve-footer with a bigger outboard, good for the ocean, and Cocó noticed how Tony and Ramón went out every morning and usually came back with a bucket filled with grunts, yellowtails and small snappers—all edible fish. When he bought a still bigger boat, with a twenty-five horsepower Mer-cury, they could go out further and catch bigger fish. Then Cocó bought the current boat. Now Cocó rarely went to the fish market in Camarioca, except when he wanted to eat lobsters.

They returned to the house around eleven with two buckets full of fish for the kitchen. Now it was time to hit the water. He loved how clear the water was on this beach. He splashed around for a while and took a turn water skiing. He skied with one ski, a slalom, and was good at it. He knew girls watched from the shore, and he liked to show off. He jumped the wake repeatedly, and once outside the wake he made sharp slalom cuts. After skiing, he went snorkeling. There was a rocky patch fifty yards in front of his house, and he could see many small but colorful fish there. Some-times he spotted lobsters, and he dove down and grabbed them.

He snorkeled for a while, then swam back to the beach and made a huge sandcastle with his siblings and his younger cousins. In Havana, he rarely spent time with them. They were on different schedules and had different interests, but on the beach, he played with them. When they finished the castle, he took his younger cousins and siblings on a walk, westward, past the last houses in that direction. They looked for seashells or baby giant sea turtles. It was a tradition with the kids on this beach to collect exotic sea-shells and keep baby turtles in the garden, in large tin pails filled with seawater.

They picked some shells and came back. He decided to go on a walk alone toward the eastern end of the beach, where the rest of the houses were located. He knew almost every person on this beach. He passed two girls his age, greeted them, but kept walking. He noticed that they were undergoing the same physical transformation that he noticed when he first saw Carmen Macía at the Yacht Club. All the girls in his group were turning into at-tractive and fully developed young women. It was unsettling. He felt he should be flirting with them, now that he was getting to the age when flirting and pairing off started, but instead he felt shier.

The section of the beach where his family lived had an active social life. Cocó's house was in a residential area called Kawama, named after the giant sea turtles that laid eggs on the beach. The neighborhood was physically distinct; one hundred large summer-houses built side-by-side on a precariously thin sliver of land with the ocean on the north and a long lagoon on the south. It was distinct in other ways, too. He had read an article in *Bohemia* that claimed that the one hundred families living in Kawama controlled half of the Cuban economy. Kawama families were the top rungs of the good families his grandmother talked about, and they owned the most visible businesses in Cuba. There was something else he thought about. Kawama residents tended to marry each other. Any girl he passed on his walk could turn out to be his future wife.

He passed some boys his age, and they shook hands and talked briefly. Those boys were destined to be either his future rivals, in love and in business, or they could also turn out to be his future business partners. And the girls, he assumed, looked at the boys on this beach and assessed how they stacked up as prospective boy-friends and husbands. They would be drawn first to their looks and their sense of humor. But later, most likely, they looked at the big picture with more calculating eyes. The boy whose father owned a bank had to look much more attractive than the boy whose fa-ther only played golf. He wondered if Carmen Macía was already thinking in those terms. He hoped not.

He kept walking and was within a few houses of his cousin Tina's house. He knew that Tina and Carmen had already arrived. He had been thinking about Carmen after he crashed into her at El Encanto. If he was going to start a proper Cuban courtship with her, he needed to summon enough courage to take a chance and make the first move. The problem was that it was hard to tell what she was thinking. He knew what he thought—that Carmen was the most attractive girl he could ever hope for, and he had a feeling that she liked him. They had shared that summer in Ciego, and she seemed to enjoy talking to him after Sunday mass. But now, it was time for him to act.

On the other hand, he didn't want to go right away to visit Car-men and appear too eager to see her. He could also predict what his aunt Nina would say when he appeared at her house:

"Oraculo," she would say, with Carmen present, "I've noticed that when Carmen is here, you can't wait to come and visit your favorite aunt. When she's not here, we never see you. I wonder what that means?"

Maybe it was too early to go and visit.

He would wait a few days. He turned around. On the walk back he noticed how the boys and girls in his group were congre-gating in front of two houses. There was a crowd talking in the water in front of Lydia Espino's house, and another group was congregating near Enrique Estrada's house. The two groups had a popularity contest.

Tony wasn't planning to spend his mornings with either group. He preferred swimming, water skiing and snorkeling in front of his house and going on walks to visit cousins, preferably with Alfredo Medina, his next door neighbor and best friend on the beach. Alfredo's family had not yet arrived.

Tony was now walking by the group at Enrique Estrada's house. He knew everyone in the water. He was thinking that he should wade in the water and shake hands with all the boys, maybe kiss the girls and stay there for a while. He was pleased to see that Tina and Carmen were not part of Enrique's group. His tendency was not to join a group. Maybe he was afraid the group would decide that he was not funny enough. There was pressure to be witty and say something funny every time someone said something. And everyone said a lot of silly things. It was too much work, being in a group. It was easier to keep walking.

His older sister Sofi did not have a problem being part of a group. A motorboat full of teenagers picked her up every morning. The boys in her group had nicknames like The Rat, The Ground Hog, Little Miss Worm, The Vulture and other outrageous names. Nicknames had a way of sticking to boys on this beach. Robertico Arteaga was in his sister's group, and he was one of the few boys they called by his real name. When their boat arrived earlier that morning, an old Cris-Craft, there were ten or fifteen members of the menagerie piled up on the boat, laughing, screaming and drinking beer. Sofi climbed on and the boat moved on, riding very low on the water. Tony always expected the boat to sink, which it did, more than once.

His parents, his aunts and uncles did not have a problem socializing either. He enjoyed watching the adults when they went on walks. Every time they crossed other residents walking in the opposite direction, his family stopped, talked to them for a while, and then kept moving until they crossed the next group of walkers. If they passed by a group standing chest deep in the water, they waved and waded into the water to join them. His mother and aunts kissed all the women, not an easy maneuver because the women all wore large straw hats—essential protection against premature wrinkles. His father and uncles kissed the women, too, and shook hands with the men. Then they split into separate groups and conversed. The women tended to form one large circle, and the men split into smaller groups.

Tony knew what the women talked about: their families, their acquaintances and their children. They were people-oriented. The men were more mysterious. Tony sometimes tried to eavesdrop to see if they talked about important things, like business deals or politics, but he rarely heard them talking about those topics. At the beach, the men liked to laugh. They told funny stories. The women laughed, too, but the men laughed louder. Drinks helped. Every day, starting at noon, portions of the beach at Kawama turned into one giant cocktail party. On his walk back to his house, he noticed that his relatives had joined the group of adults in front of Arturo de Meyer's house. He waved at them, and they waved back. He watched Suarez, Arturo's butler, dressed in a white linen jacket and a bathing suit, wading into the ocean holding up a large silver tray filled with drinks and hors d'oeuvres. The adults in his house joined two or three groups like that every day before their walk was over. When they came home for lunch, everyone was tipsy.

LUNCH at Cocó's was served at two. After the first morning on the beach, the family was hungry. The adults were in an especially cheerful mood. They exchanged the information they had gathered during their morning walk and the various wade-in cock-tail parties—who was looking terrible, who had gained or lost weight, who had bought a new yacht. They recounted some of the funnier stories they had heard. The fish was brought in, and Tony got some praise. He had caught some good-sized red snappers, everyone's favorite fish. After lunch, everyone went to his or her rooms for their daily naps.

His father once told him that he was the result of a nap. He thought about that statement as he watched all the adults moving toward their bedrooms. He headed for his favorite spot, the couch on the porch. From that couch, he had a good view of the ocean. The breeze picked up around three, and it felt good.

He also liked to watch the servants. Many congregated in the water in front of Cocó's house. At naptime, the servants and the nannies were free. He could tell this was their favorite time of the day. There was a lot of laughing and water splashing. He noticed that Gonzalo was back to his old tricks, teaching a new maid from another house how to swim. The lessons consisted of Gonzalo holding up the student so she could practice her strokes. Gonzalo's lesson involved a lot of touching, but there was also much laugh-ing, and the new maid did not seem to mind.

The servants also got together at night, when their duties were over, in the thatch-roofed lagoon docks. They would open a bottle of rum, and someone would bring a guitar. He knew the servants in his house looked forward all year to the summer on Varadero Beach.

He woke up from his nap around five, and a new round of activities started. Tony went out trolling for little barracudas in the lagoon. His family had a little boat with a small outboard an-chored by the lagoon dock just for that purpose. The barracudas served as bait for the morning fishing trip. He came back with a bucket filled with small barracudas and put them in the freezer. The adults woke up and went out to play golf, bridge or canasta. He bicycled to Club Kawama to play tennis with a group of de la Torre cousins who lived nearby. That night, the adults went to a dinner party. His sister Sofi went out to visit Lola de Armas, one of the popular girls in her group. He ate a light dinner with the younger children on the porch; fish soup, plantains, rice and black beans. After dinner, they played monopoly.

Tony followed this daily routine—what he had always done on this beach—for one week. He figured he was reverting to his old self and had forgotten all of Mr. Eloy's lessons or Gonzalo's advice about being a doer because he kept postponing his visit to Carmen. Then Alfredo arrived.

15

THE MORNING AFTER THE MEDINAS
got in, Tony decided to skip fishing and spend the morning with
Alfredo. He slept late, ate breakfast and walked next door to the
Medinas' house, where he found Alfredo finishing his breakfast at
a table set on their porch. Alfredo had been his fishing and skiing
partner as long as he could remember, but last summer Alfredo
had lost interest in fishing and had become more interested in girls.

Alfredo was half a year older than Tony, but in many ways,
he seemed much older. He was much taller than Tony and more
cynical. He had just finished his first year at Andover, an American prep school, and Tony was eager to hear what he had to say
about going to an American school. He had already heard one
story, when Alfredo returned to Havana for Christmas. His Andover roommate had invited him for Thanksgiving at his home in

Boston, and that weekend they crashed a party that some older kids were throwing. Alfredo and his roommate had gotten drunk and were asked to leave, which they did, but not before Alfredo had urinated in the punch bowl.

Alfredo got up from the table and greeted Tony: "Antonio, *Coño*, how are you?" They shook hands. For some reason, he was the only person Tony knew who called him Antonio. He liked that. Antonio sounded like the name of an older, more sophisticated person.

"Antonio, I was going down to the beach to do some water skiing. Join me."

The Medinas had a Chris Craft, and Orlando, their driver, was sitting on the boat, ready to go.

They went down to the beach and dove in. The day was overcast. The water felt cold.

"So tell me about Andover," Tony said.

"I hate it," Alfredo said, laughing.

"Why?"

"There is nothing to do except study."

"Didn't you meet some American girls?"

"Not at Andover. They have two dances a year, but you have to be a junior or senior to invite a girl over for the weekend. Choate is going to be the same. You are going to spend the year with five hundred very horny boys. Get ready to jerk off a lot."

"You must have had at least one date!"

"I did, when I went with my roommate to his house in Boston."

"When you pissed in the punch bowl!"

Alfredo laughed. "That was not one of my finer moments, but the next day I got fixed up with a blind date. We went to a drive-in movie. We necked during the entire movie. I can't even tell you what movie was playing."

So here was another confirmation about the dating habits of American girls. Now that he was giving up on brothels, he thought that he better meet an American girl if he had any hopes of having any physical contact with the opposite sex. Carmen, and all the other Cuban girls in his group, were hopeless on that front.

He had a sudden inspiration. There were many American girls vacationing every summer on Varadero Beach, and most of them stayed at the Internacional, the modern hotel at the eastern end of the beach. They could ski to the Internacional, go to the pool and try to meet some vacationing American girls. The older boys went to the pool at the Internacional every day. He suggested this idea to Alfredo.

"Antonio, I'm shocked. The last time I saw you, you were only interested in fishing. Yes, let's give the Internacional a shot. I cannot believe this, the water this morning feels cold. I need to warm up. My parents are still sleeping, and I know where they keep the cognac."

Tony thought: Why not? He had enjoyed having the Cuba Libres at the Mambo. Drinks made him braver. They went back to the house. Alfredo produced the bottle from a bar on the terrace. He took a swig.

"*Coño*," he said. "This is very good Cognac, the best French Cognac. It's very strong stuff. Try it." He passed the bottle to Tony.

Coño had to be the most popular Cuban swear word. No one knew what it meant. Tony took a swig.

"*Coño*," Tony said. "It tastes awful."

"But it feels good," Alfredo said, laughing. He reached for the bottle, gulped down two more swigs and passed it back to Tony.

It didn't taste so bad the second time. He took a few good swigs. He was starting to feel dizzy.

"I'll have some more," Alfredo said.

Julio, Alfredo's older brother, came out from the living room, where he had been playing the piano. He had just graduated from Andover and was going to enter Yale in September, a big deal because that's where Alfredo's father had gone to college during the same years when Tony's father and his brothers were there. Julio wore glasses and was shorter than Alfredo. In many ways, he was Alfredo's exact opposite. He was a rare individual on Varadero beach—a practicing intellectual. He didn't water ski, didn't fish, didn't seem too interested in girls and thought that the other boys in his age group were total idiots. Julio got up early every morning and read philosophy books, played classical piano, spoke in English half the time and was appalled by Cuban high society and their total lack of interest in anything cultural.

The boys in his age group thought Julio was *pájaro*, a polite term for gay, if only because he was different. Tony liked Julio. He was irreverent and funny. Tony admired the fact that Julio was smart, had done well at Andover and had been accepted to Yale. Julio had done what Tony was supposed to do. Tony knew that he was expected to continue the family tradition and go to Yale.

"Antonio, good morning," Julio said, cheerfully. "Isn't it a bit early for the two delinquents to be gulping down liquor? Antonio, I heard Choate accepted you. Congratulations. Did your grandfather Cocó promise to donate a new building?"

"Julio," Alfredo said, laughing. "All they could get from Cocó was an offer to buy the toilet paper for the gym."

"So what are the two morons doing this morning?"

"Julio," Tony said. "The only thing we know we are not going to do is read a philosophy book!"

"Antonio," Julio said. "You are such an idiot. When was the last time you read a book?"

"As a matter of fact, Julio, in the past six months I must have read over twenty novels."

This was true. During the past year, Gonzalo passed on to Tony his entire collection of cheaply printed and badly written pornographic novels. They were so badly written that they were funny.

"I can't believe it," Julio said. "Congratulations. Maybe there is some hope for you. Who are you reading?"

"Julio, I don't think you'll recognize the authors. They're Cubans."

"Oh my God! He's reading Cuban literature! Antonio, it looks like you'll turn out to be a moron after all. I hate to tell you, but Cuba hasn't produced one writer worth reading."

"Julio," Alfredo broke in, laughing. "You are such an incredible *comemierda*!"

A shit eater.

"Antonio," Alfredo said. "Let's go. Don't waste your time talking to my very boring brother. Have one more swig. Hey, before we go, let's take a look at the Internacional."

Alfredo had a reflector telescope set on the balcony off his bedroom, an expensive contraption designed for star gazing and purchased for that purpose and the advancement of Alfredo's education, but the telescope had rarely been aimed at the moons of Jupiter or the rings of Saturn. Alfredo mostly used it to focus on the girls on the beach. They went up to Alfredo's porch and checked out the beachfront by the Internacional. They could see a few girls sunbathing. Tony aimed the telescope in another direction. He was curious to see who was swimming in front of his cousin Tina's house. It was amazing how clearly he could see everyone there, and he could see that Tina and Carmen were already in the water, talking with a group of boys. He knew that he had to get over there soon.

Down on the beach, Tony felt dizzy. It was a nice feeling. He ran across the sand and somersaulted into the ocean. The water felt good. Everything felt good.

Orlando was ready for them. He started the boat and brought

it near, idled it, jumped to the back and threw two slaloms and two towropes in their direction. He jumped into the driver's seat, engaged the boat forward, waited until the slaloms were on and the towropes were taut. Orlando gunned the boat, and they were off.

Alfredo was either drunk or close to it. He was screaming, laughing, jumping the wake and yelling "Fire!" Alfredo yelled "Fire!" whenever he felt exuberant. He did this often. He probably yelled "Fire!" when he pissed on the punchbowl in Boston. Tony was feeling very athletic, cutting sharp slalom turns, shooting fan-like sprays of water in the opposite direction. He imagined all the girls on the shore looking in his direction and asking: "Who is that terrific skier?"

As they passed Lydia Espino's house and her group in the water, he felt like showing off. He shot out the wake and did an extra sharp turn, his shoulder almost parallel to the water. He did the cut so well he decided to do it again when they passed the Estrada house, but his first cut was way too sharp, and he fell—a total wipeout! How embarrassing! Everyone must have been watching because when he surfaced he could hear the group by the Estrada's clapping and laughing. Orlando seemed to take forever to turn the boat around and pass the towrope by him. He grabbed it, Orlando gunned the boat, and they were off again.

When they passed by Tina Campos' house, he decided to stay behind the boat and not risk another fall. He looked toward the house and saw Tina, Carmen and the boys in the water. He had to go over there tomorrow. No more hesitation. He waved at them, and the group waved back.

They were now getting closer to the center of the town of Varadero and the long row of five story wooden hotels built by the water. Cuban middle class families from all over the island stayed in those hotels. As they approached the town, the seascape changed. There were more and more people in the water, as well as many small boats. Many were rented rowboats, filled with families from small towns in the provinces, possibly venturing out on the ocean for the first time. These families became Alfredo's targets. He pulled on his towrope and passed under Tony's rope, so now he was on the land's side. As Orlando passed close to the rowboats, Alfredo shot out of the wake, aimed straight at the horrified rowers, and just before hitting them, he turned sharply on the slalom, soaking everyone. He did this every chance he got, yelling "Fire!" before every water attack.

Tony was thinking that Alfredo's water attacks were cruel, but then, he figured a little water could not hurt anyone. He spotted a rowboat ahead on the ocean side. He would also go outside the wake and soak them. He had never done anything like that before. He saw that his target was a family. There were kids, and a woman was holding up an umbrella to protect her from the sun. The umbrella would come in handy to keep her dry because it was going to pour. He shot out from the wake and aimed for the rowboat. He could see the family staring at him. As he got closer, he realized that he did not have it in him. It did not feel right to soak them. He quickly moved back inside the wake and watched the family go by. He waved at them, and they waved back.

The Batista compound was located a few houses before the Hotel Internacional. There were usually two navy patrol boats anchored there with many bored looking soldiers on deck, all holding machine guns. Tony suddenly panicked. He could envision a serious accident. Maybe Alfredo was so drunk that he was going to take a cut at the soldiers, yell "Fire!" and soak them. Who could predict how the bored and ignorant soldiers from the interior would react?

But Alfredo must have sobered up quickly. He came back inside the wake and was a model of propriety as they passed the patrol boats. They waved at the soldiers, who stared back with a blank expression. At the Internacional, they shot outside of the wake, aimed for the beach and let go of the tows.

They waded up to the sand. The girls they had seen through the telescope were still there, lying face up on beach towels, sunbathing. Closer up they seemed too old for them. They looked around for girls closer to their age, but they could not see any.

The girls on the sand were probably American college students or secretaries from Miami. Those girls were the perfect targets for the boys in Tony's sister's group. The older boys came to the nightclub at the Internacional after they dropped off their Cuban dates and asked the American tourists to dance. They usually said yes, since they came to Cuba to have fun and dancing the Mambo or the cha-cha-chá was something they never did in New York. The Cuban boys were more than glad to give them Mambo lessons, but they were after the ultimate good luck—picking up an American girl who would sleep with them.

Nothing close to that was going to happen with the Cuban girls in their group. Cuban girls were impossible to kiss or neck with. Necking with a Cuban girl seemed beyond the realm of the possible. The nuns had them all brainwashed. Even if, by a small miracle, a Cuban girl was interested in being naughty, the logistics made necking or kissing very difficult. Chaperones always hovered about. Other girls and boys hovered about, since teenagers on this beach did everything in groups. It was nearly impossible to find yourself alone with a Cuban girl.

"Antonio," Alfredo said. "Let's give these girls a try."

"Alfredo," Tony said. "Those girls are 20, 21 years old."

"Antonio, so what? We'll tell them we're older." I'll take the tall one, and you take the short one.

"Fine," Tony said. "I'll let you talk." Clearly, it was not going to work. But he was still a little drunk and brave, and Alfredo had prepared for this in prep school.

They walked up to the pair: "Good morning girls," Alfredo said. "How are you?"

They looked up, a bit surprised.

"We're fine," said the one Alfredo had picked for himself.

"You sure look fine," Alfredo said.

Not a bad line, Tony thought, but maybe it sounded funny, coming from a fourteen-year-old.

"My friend and I," Alfredo continued. "We thought you might want to water ski. That's our boat anchored there. We would be delighted to take you out for a spin."

"Oh, that's very nice," Alfredo's girl continued. She seemed amused. "You boys live on Varadero Beach?"

"Yes," Alfredo said. "But we go to school in the States."

"Oh, where?"

"We go to Choate, a prep school in Connecticut. We're seniors," Tony said, relieving the pressure he was feeling about needing to say something.

"You don't look like seniors to me." She seemed amused.

"Actually, we are not seniors yet, but we'll be seniors soon," Alfredo said. "So, what do you say? Do you want to go water skiing?"

"That's very nice of you, but we're from New York, and we only ski on snow," the other girl said.

"That is not a problem," Alfredo said. "Going from skiing on snow to skiing on water is a cinch. Especially if you have excellent instructors like us to teach you. I'm Alfredo. This is my friend Antonio. So what are your names?"

"No, no, no!" Alfredo's girl said, laughing. "We're almost twice your age. Are all Cuban men sexual maniacs?"

"Please!" Alfredo said, pretending to be hurt. "Sexual maniacs!

We're just trying to be hospitable!" Then Alfredo turned toward Tony: "Sexual maniacs! Antonio, you've been discovered!"

"Please, go bother someone else." Alfredo's girl said. She went back to reading.

They got the message and walked back toward their boat. Alfredo repeated once more, "Sexual maniacs!" and laughed. Tony was thinking that she was probably right about Cuban men being sexual maniacs. They climbed on the boat and rode with Orlando on the trip back.

Still, Tony felt mildly pleased. They struck out, but at least they had tried.

16

THE NEXT MORNING TONY WENT
fishing with Ramón. He noticed that his mind kept wandering—
thinking about what else he could be doing. Instead of fishing,
he could be scouting the beach at the Internacional, looking for
American girls. It seemed so easy—to simply walk up to an American girl and start talking. He was also thinking about Carmen. It
was ridiculous, liking a girl and being afraid to visit her. Emilio
would not have hesitated for one second. He would have gone to
her house the first day. Alfredo, too. In fact, that morning, Alfredo
was visiting Eugenia Sanchez, the girl he liked. She was witty and
exceptionally tall. They were made for each other.

Tony needed to walk to Tina's house and spend the morning
talking to Carmen. But, he thought, talking about what? So he kept
putting it off, and here he was, fishing.

Too often he suffered from a surprising lack of self-confidence. He was afraid that if Carmen got to know him, she would find him boring, or stupid, or shy, or not good enough for her or all of the above. But then he thought how, as a child, everyone always told him that he had beautiful blue eyes and how he usually replied: yes, I know. And his eyes hadn't changed, so he still had that going for him. And now he thought about all he had learned lately about being forward, from Emilio, Gonzalo and Alfredo. He should be feeling more confident. Whenever he felt he needed to push himself and do something that required some courage, the poem that Mr. Eloy had recited came to mind. He liked it so much, he had memorized it: *Storm'd at with shot and shell, Boldly they rode and well, Into the jaws of Death, Into the mouth of Hell, Rode the six hundred.* He decided to stop procrastinating and visit Carmen later that morning.

WHEN he got back to his house, he started on the walk up the beach to Tina's house. On the way over he ignored everyone he knew, barely waving at them. He was intensely focused on the problem at hand—what he was going to talk about with Carmen. He never had a problem talking to boys, but with girls, he was tongue-tied. He had a feeling that, with girls, he should be more personal. He should tell Carmen that he thought she was very attractive and also that he liked her. She might be really impressed by his honesty. But, more likely, if he said anything like that, Carmen would laugh out loud. Then she would lose all interest in him and move on to having fantasies about someone else, someone who was more of a challenge. Maybe as an older person, one could be more honest and direct, but right now, at his age, it was tricky. He had to strike a fine line. He had to let Carmen know he liked her, but he had to keep her guessing how much he liked her. But then, if he was too casual with her and came across as uninterested, that would not be good, either. She would lose all interest in him. Courting a girl at his age was complicated. Girls were complicated.

As he approached Tina's house, he could see a small group in the water. He felt a sinking feeling. The group included Carmen, Tina and four boys! The boys were splashing water at the girls. How infantile! This scene was not part of the plan, but he couldn't turn back now. He walked up to the group and waded in. He now saw that one of the boys was Luis, Tina's younger brother, and another was a friend of Luis. Those did not count. But the other two boys were Tony's age. The Godoy brothers. They lived nearby. They were there to flirt with Tina and Carmen.

"Oraculo," Tina said. "We were wondering when you were going to pay us a visit."

Tony went up to her and kissed her.

"Hello Carmen," he said, turning to Carmen, maybe too enthusiastically. He was unsure whether he should kiss her or shake hands, so he did neither. He greeted his cousin Luis and his friend and shook hands with the Godoys.

"So what brings you to this part of the world," Carmen said, smiling.

God, Tony thought, don't you know? To see you.

"I wanted to drop by and say hello and see how you are doing." There. An honest statement.

"I'm doing well," Carmen said. "Although right now, at this very moment, I'm being bitten on my foot by tiny sardines."

"Sardines do that for some reason," Tony said. Gonzalo would have said: "I would give anything to be a sardine."

"Sardines like stinky feet," one of the Godoy boys said.

Carmen laughed and splashed him.

"Did you hear what happened to my cousin Ana María the other day?" the other boy said. Tony could tell he was going to have trouble getting in a word with these two around.

"What happened?" Carmen said.

"She got bitten on her wrist by a barracuda, right in front of her house."

"No!" Carmen yelled.

"Yes, she had four stitches. She was wearing a silver bracelet, and a barracuda struck it. They think anything that shines is a sardine."

"That's awful," Carmen said. "I'm wearing a ring." She raised her hand and showed Tony her ring. "Do you think I'm in danger?"

"Don't worry," Tony said. "The worse that could happen is that you end up with four fingers."

"You're terrible!" Carmen said and splashed him.

Then one of the older boys exclaimed: "I'm a barracuda!" He dove under and swam toward Carmen. She moved away, laughing and said: "Get Away!"

Then the Godoys started splashing water at the girls again. Tony could tell that his first official visit to a girl was turning into a disaster. He reluctantly joined in the water splashing. He cheered up a little, though, when he noticed that Carmen was splashing more water toward him than toward the other boys.

Before he left he came up with a brilliant idea, a way of seeing Carmen without having to compete with these boys. He suggested that he and Luis take on Carmen and Tina at doubles tennis. They could play at Club Kawama that afternoon, at five, when it was not so hot.

CLUB Kawama marked the eastern edge of the Kawama neighborhood. It was not so much a club as it was a small hotel with a restaurant, bar and a dozen upscale rental cottages set in a pine grove. Tony went there mostly to play tennis and to gawk at the occasional Hollywood stars that rented the cottages. The beach-side bar was very popular, both at the noon hour, when bathers came in for drinks, and at night, when a popular trio played. This was a favorite spot for the older boys when they took Kawama girls out on dates. Club Kawama was also famous for Ava Gardner sightings. The rumor about Ava Gardner was that she was sexually promiscuous and obsessed with Spanish matadors and Cuban lovers. She rented a cottage at Club Kawama every year, and when she did, stories made the rounds about the wild parties at her cottage.

Tina's house was only four houses away from the club so Luis and the girls walked. Tony bicycled from his house. They met at the court at five and played for an hour. Tony got interested in tennis at Camp Pasquaney, and after that, he kept playing. He was thinking he might play at Choate. Luis was the worst player of the foursome, but Carmen and Tina were decent players. Tía Nina had insisted that her daughter play sports, so she would have a good figure. Tina and Carmen ended up taking lessons together at the Vedado Tennis Club and started to enjoy the game. Luis and Tony, the worst and the best players, were paired against Carmen and Tina. If they kept the ball on Luis' side of the court, the girls could win some points.

Tony and Luis played in their bathing suits, without shirts. The girls came wearing cute white shorts and white polo shirts. Tony noticed how Carmen's very shapely tanned legs stood out in all that white. She was a good player. She ran fast and hit the ball with decent form. She also wanted to win. Her athleticism was very sexy. Whenever the ball came to him, he hit it back to Carmen, and she hit it back to him. They bantered and laughed after extended rallies. Every time he made a good shot and won the point, Carmen said, "Nice shot!" He really liked getting the "Nice Shot!" comments from her.

After the game, they went to the outdoor terrace next to the bar and ordered cokes. Tina mentioned that many of the mothers were encouraging the girls in their group to plan a dance party, but no one wanted to give the first party. She had heard that Lydia Espino might do it. When they finished their cokes, they agreed to play every day.

The afternoon doubles tennis game at Club Kawama became part of his summer schedule. His conversations with Carmen after the games always felt short of what he was looking for—a hint from Carmen that he was more to her than just an acquaintance and a tennis partner. Mostly, they talked about the standard subject of Cuban high society—gossip about others.

Carmen, Tina and Tony had one thing in common: they were all starting school in the US in September. Tina was going to Foxcroft, a horsy school in Virginia where Tía Nina had gone, and Carmen was going to Kenwood, a girl's Catholic school in Albany. No one seemed too nervous about going away to school in another country. The Cuban upper class studied in the United States. Their parents had done it, and now it was their turn. In a way, going away to school was exciting—a move toward independence and adulthood. Tony made a mental note to find a map and check the distance between Albany and Wallingford. He was hoping those cities were not too far apart. He could take a train from Choate to Albany and visit Carmen. He had already determined that he was going to visit Carmen in the winter. They could go sledding together, then build a snowman, then have a snowball fight—the American equivalent of splashing water at each other. One thought was especially intriguing: he wondered how much the behavior of Cuban girls would change up north when they went out on a date without a chaperone.

HE turned fourteen at the end of the month, and his mother wanted him to give a small dinner party. She suggested he invite around ten or twelve boys and girls from his group. They could set tables in the garden, prepare a meal and hire a trio. Tony didn't like the suggestion. He didn't feel comfortable being the center of attention at any party, no matter how small. Instead, he wanted to rent a fishing boat with a captain and go night deep-sea fishing with Alfredo and two of his de la Torre cousins. His mother finally gave in. Alfredo brought with him a brand new Cognac bottle. They all got giddy, but also managed to catch a dozen large red snappers.

17

TONY WOKE UP THINKING ABOUT Albany. If someone had an atlas on Varadero Beach, it had to be Julio. He quickly ate breakfast and went next door to the Medinas' house. Julio was playing the piano at eight in the morning! Julio seemed surprised by Tony's request. Sure, he had an atlas. They walked up to Julio's room. He had a wall full of books and quickly found his atlas. It was impressive, how many books Julio had read, and this was his bookshelf in his family's summer home. The one in his house in Havana was undoubtedly larger. It was scary, too; in the next few years, at Choate, he might also have to read a wall full of books and remember their contents.

He opened the atlas to the US map and was disappointed to see that Albany, New York, was a good distance from Wallingford, Connecticut. He did notice that New York City was in the middle, and both Carmen and he had to pass by New York City on their way to school and on their way back to Cuba. They could meet in the city, maybe at the top of the Empire State Building.

Alfredo had heard him talking to Julio. He yelled for Tony to come to his room.

He was looking through the telescope. "Antonio, look at this," he said.

Tony looked. He could see two girls sitting on towels on the beach in front of the Internacional.

Alfredo looked again. "Those are new girls," he said "Great legs. Let's go. Fire!"

Sure, Tony thought. Let's go.

They went down to the water, climbed on the boat and took off for the Internacional. When they got there, they saw that the girls were still there, now lying on beach towels close to the surf. One was lying on her side reading a book, the other was lying on her back, sunbathing.

"Let's take a good look," Alfredo said.

They walked by the girls, and kept walking for a short distance, then sat down on the sand and stared at the ocean.

"They are close to our age," Tony said.

"Let's talk to them!" Alfredo said.

They got up and walked back. Alfredo kneeled down on the sand in front of the girl reading. Tony stood by.

"Hello!" Alfredo said.

The girl looked up from her book. She must have found him adequate.

"Hello!" she said.

"We've been waiting for you all summer." Alfredo said.

"Well, here we are! What do we do now?"

Tony laughed. Even Alfredo was surprised. The other girl sat up and seemed interested.

Alfredo continued: "Would you like to go water-skiing?"

"That's our boat over there," Tony said.

"Nice boat! I wouldn't mind water-skiing." She smiled.

"Hey, let's go," Alfredo said.

"I'm Tony, and he's Alfredo. What are your names?"

"Wait a minute," she said. "We need to confer." They got up and moved out of earshot. Their conference was punctuated by a few laughs and by occasional glances in their direction. They came back.

"Let's do it," the girl who had been talking said. "But it has to be a short ride. Sarah's parents are still in bed, and they won't be too happy if they can't find us when they come out to the beach."

Tony had been watching Sarah. She still had not said a word, but she seemed to be amused by the proceedings. She struck Tony as a classic American girl. Blond, blue-eyed, with a perfect nose and a slender body. She looked like a young Grace Kelly, a beautiful new actress who had starred in *High Noon* and *Mogambo*.

"Now we know Sarah's name," Alfredo said. "But we don't know your name, dear."

"My name is Alexandra. Alex for short. 'Dear' sounds good too."

They started walking toward the boat. Alfredo was walking next to Alex, and they continued talking. Sarah walked next to Tony. At first, he did not know what to say. This was his first conversation with an American girl. He was nervous. Finally, he asked her where she was from. She said she lived in Philadelphia, and she and Alex went to a private school there called the Friends. He told her he was going to Choate in September, and Sarah perked up. She knew Choate. A friend from Philadelphia had started at Choate last year. He seemed to really like the school. That got them going.

They waded in and approached the boat. Alfredo told Orlando that he could take a break and go for a swim; they were taking the girls water-skiing. Tony was thinking that American girls were gutsy. A new kind of girl. Cuban girls would never go out skiing alone with a pair of boys they had just met, but these girls did not hesitate.

Alfredo and Alex took the first turn skiing. Tony drove the boat eastward, past the last house in that direction, the DuPont mansion. It belonged to Irene DuPont, an eccentric American millionaire. Tony figured he started acting eccentric the moment his mother named him Irene. He had never seen him, but he owned the entire eastern end of the Hicacos Peninsula, seven or eight miles of it, and he never socialized with anyone, especially anyone Cuban. As a concession, he allowed the natives to play on his professional eighteen-hole golf course if they did not mind waiting for the iguanas to move off the greens. Mr. DuPont loved iguanas, and his staff fed them. Hundreds of these huge lizards roamed the golf course. Tony's father played golf there every afternoon.

Tony told Sarah about Irene DuPont and about the golf course populated by the iguanas. Sarah said she would like to see the iguanas. No problem, Tony assured her. Sarah sat next to him on the front seat, and she turned to look back toward the skiers. Tony kept alternating between looking forward and looking backward and was stealing quick glances at Sarah in the process. She was pretty. Her eyes were striking—a much brighter shade of blue than his.

The motor noise seemed too loud for talking so they focused on the skiers. Alex was a good skier; she and Alfredo were jumping in and out of the wake. After they passed the DuPont mansion, Alfredo made signs for him to get close to the beach—they were getting off.

From here to the end of the peninsula, there were no houses, no bathers, and no access roads. Only miles of virgin beach, coconut trees, clear water and iguanas; a perfect tourist postcard. The skiers let go of the tow. Tony turned the boat around and anchored it close to Alex and Alfredo. Tony and Sarah jumped in. Tony suspected that Alfredo's intention was to attempt to get into a necking session here. It seemed too quick for that, but then, Alfredo was the expert on American girls. Tony was relieved when they started a normal conversation about their impressions of Cuba, about Philadelphia, about school. Then Sarah focused everyone's attention on a few large iguanas sunning themselves at the edge of the foliage. The large lizards stared at them, but did not move. People did not scare them.

"The iguanas are amazing," Sarah said. "They look prehistoric."

"They're like sharks, unchanged after millions of years," Tony said.

"I can see why sharks haven't changed," Sarah said. "No fish can eat them in the ocean, but why did the iguanas survive?"

That was a good question. Tony had no idea why the iguanas survived.

"Maybe because they're so ugly! They don't look appetizing," Alfredo said.

"I wonder," Sarah said. "How does one iguana decide when another iguana is sexy?"

"If they are the opposite sex, and they are alive!" Tony ventured. They all laughed.

They bantered some more about the iguanas and walked on the beach looking for seashells. Then Sarah said: "I think we better go back. My parents might be up and looking for us."

"Okay," Tony said, and he surprised himself when he quickly blurted out: "But we would like to see you again. Can we see you again tonight?"

"Yes, definitely," Alfredo piped in quickly.

"We might be able to arrange something," Alex said. "After all, you've been waiting for us all summer."

"Absolutely," Alfredo said.

"It's true," Tony said. For once, it was.

They all climbed in the boat and drove back to the Internacional. When they got there, Sarah surprised them.

"Look," she said. "My dad has one rule: no socializing with the local boys. Don't look so sad. We can get around it, as long as they don't see us with you. We have dinner with my parents every night, but after dinner, they go to the casino, and we're on our own. We can meet you at the downtown square. We'll talk to them tonight about going to the square. Meet us at the hotel's beach again at the same time tomorrow morning, and we'll have a plan for tomorrow night."

"Hey, we'll be there tomorrow," Alfredo said.

"Yes, same time," Tony said.

The girls got off the boat and swam to the shore. Tony and Alfredo looked at each other and grinned, amazed by their good fortune. Orlando climbed aboard and drove them back to Kawama. He had a good idea why Alfredo kept yelling: "Fire! Fire!" and Tony kept repeating: *"Coño! Coñooo! Coñoooooooo!"*

When the boat sped by Tina's house, he didn't even look in that direction.

H E found it impossible to fall asleep after lunch. It looked like he would soon go out on a date with an American girl. He was thinking how Sarah had offered to come up with a strategy to get away from her parents. Sarah was a new kind of girl—a girl who thought like a boy. All she wanted, after all, was to slip away from parental supervision and explore life on her own. He could imagine her that night at dinner, talking amiably to her parents, searching for the

flaws in the parental rules designed to keep their daughter virtu-
ous, safe and at an arm's length from the Cuban boys.

When it got close to five, he got on his bicycle and headed for
Club Kawama. He was enjoying his tennis ritual with Carmen, and
it did not occur to him that his new interest in Sarah conflicted in
any way with his interest in Carmen. He didn't think he was being
deceitful. They were simply two different girls, in two different
time slots and in two different worlds. He would see Sarah in the
evening and Carmen in the afternoon. Carmen was a long-term
romantic project. He had no plans to try to kiss Carmen in the
next few years. He could wait to do that, which was what Cuban
men had always done. But he was going to try to kiss Sarah within
the next few days, and maybe he would try for more, like the older
boys.

He was very pleased with his newfound theory on how he
could be interested in Carmen and Sarah at the same time. But
his Carmen for Romance, Sarah for Sex theory didn't seem to work
in practice. Carmen had a new tennis outfit on, a short white skirt
that came down just above her knees. The new skirt was much sex-
ier than the shorts she had on the previous day. As she ran around
the court and swung at the ball, the skirt flew up at times and
revealed, during an erotic split second, her well-formed thighs.

After the game, they had a different kind of conversation. Tony
knew that Carmen was interested in politics. At the University of
Havana, where her mother taught, the students were always dem-
onstrating or rioting about politics. He assumed that in Carmen's
house, politics was part of the dinner conversation. Tony's interest in politics was non-existent. At times, he heard the servants
talk about politics, but Cocó had one rule at the family dinner
table. He did not want to hear any discussions about politics. Cocó
claimed that he had always thrived in business because he didn't

take sides in politics. He viewed all politicians as corrupt or worse, and it had served him well to always stay clear of them.

The conversation had started with the latest gossip on the beach: Batista had arrived at Varadero for an extended vacation, and he had invited many Kawama residents to a dinner party, placing them in a delicate social quandary. Apparently, some families did not want to go, and Tony suspected the reasons—besides being an illegal president, he came from another social class altogether, and he was mulatto. All the families listed in the Social Guide were white. But many families had accepted the invitation anyway. The consensus was that it was a very bad idea to reject an invitation from the president of the republic.

"I don't see how accepting his invitation is a problem," Tina said.

"Because it's wrong," Carmen said.

"Carmen," Tony asked. "Why is it wrong?"

"Because he seized power illegally. Dictators are never good. Machado, our last dictator, stole, killed and ruined the Cuban economy. Most families in Kawama don't seem too concerned about Batista, but they should be. Batista hasn't stolen or killed or ruined the Cuban economy yet, but he will."

Tony did not know what to say. He didn't think at all about Batista or the Cuban economy. Those seemed to be strictly adult topics.

THE next morning, he and Alfredo had breakfast together, then skied to the Internacional. There was one thing that Batista had done that bothered Tony; he had extended the buoys into deeper water in front of his compound. For security reasons, they did not want any boats or swimmers there. When they skied past his house on the way to the Internacional, the boat had to turn into deep ocean to bypass the Batista buoys. Tony didn't like skiing over dark blue water. If he fell, there could be some big sharks under him.

At the Internacional, they anchored and stayed on the boat until the girls came out. They told them that Sarah's parents were already up so Tony and Alfredo had to leave quickly, but it was all worked out. They had permission to go to the movie house that night in the main square. They could meet them there around eight, and they could see the movie or do something else.

BACK in Alfredo's room, they kept focusing on what Sarah had said: they could see the movie or do something else. They went over the options. They did not want to see a movie. They should go someplace where they could talk, get to know them and then neck. They could hang around in the park or go bowling. Those were good activities for getting acquainted, but not private enough to do anything else. Alfredo thought that their best option was to have Orlando drive them around on a scenic tour. He would bring a cognac bottle, and they could drive around and talk, get drunk, and then they could neck. They could take them on a ride to Cardenas, a nearby quaint, sleepy port town, or go to the Pines, a mysterious stretch of beach on the road to Matanzas. The Pines was also known as the Cemetery of the Kawamas. For some inexplicable reason, giant sea turtles went to that strip of beach to die.

Tony liked the turtle idea best. The Pines was an eerie place at night, with a hundred large Kawama carcasses glowing in the moonlight. This was a perfect place to take the girls—a scary, secluded place, and Sarah seemed to have an interest in the local fauna. Once that was settled, Alfredo went downstairs and asked his dad if he could use Orlando and the car that evening. He offered the standard lie—that he and Tony wanted to see a movie playing in Cardenas.

18

TONY AND ALFREDO ARRIVED
ahead of time in Alfredo's father's black Cadillac. Alfredo's dad
was the Cuban distributor for Cadillacs and other GM cars. His
Cadillac was a special model with a small bar built into the back of
the front seats. Orlando parked the car next to the movie theater.
Before they got out of the car, Alfredo opened a cognac bottle and
filled two shot glasses.

"To American girls," he toasted.

"To a date without chaperones," Tony replied.

They gulped the drinks down, got out of the car, crossed
the street and sat on a bench at the edge of the park. The town
of Varadero was not unlike other small Cuban towns Tony had
seen, with the church and the municipal building anchoring the
two ends of the central park, and a wooden gazebo in the center,

where a band played on festive occasions. Shops surrounded the park. Tourist shops selling straw hats and local crafts, an ice cream shop, a few restaurants, one movie theater and La Bolera, a modest nightclub.

The social life of the town was taking place in the park itself. The unattached girls of the town were walking around the park in groups, clockwise, while the unattached boys were going around counterclockwise. When a boy wanted to court a girl, he asked her to walk with him, or they sat down on a bench in the center of the park and talked. The girl's parents and the rest of the town sat on other benches and watched the evolving courtships.

Sarah and Alex arrived on foot. They were wearing light summer dresses, fitted to the waist, with thin straps holding the top. The girls laughed when they were led to the car with the uniformed chauffeur and seemed impressed when they all squeezed into the back seat and Alfredo passed around shot glasses. He poured some Cognac into each glass.

"A toast," Alfredo said, raising his glass. "To a tropical date!"

The girls did not seem to hesitate at all. They gulped down their drinks.

"How about another toast!" Tony offered.

"Okay, you make one," Sarah said.

Alfredo served everyone again. Tony thought Sarah was testing him. He had to come up with a good toast. One thing he learned from Gonzalo was that women liked compliments, even when they were blatant lies. He had trouble lying, so his compliment had to be truthful. He raised his glass:

"To two beautiful girls from Philadelphia and to two lucky guys from Havana!"

Sarah and Alex laughed again. They gulped down the second shot. Tony was impressed. These girls were not novices at drinking.

"I liked your toast, but why do you feel you are lucky guys?" Alex asked Tony, playfully.

"Hey," Alfredo broke in, laughing. "We're lucky to be rich and smart and good looking."

Alfredo was not prone to modesty, and his intention was to make them laugh, but that toast rang true to Tony. They were lucky to be rich, a much more preferable situation to being poor, and maybe they were smart. He did not know about the good-looking part.

Still, Tony felt he should improve Alfredo's toast: "We're lucky to have met you," he said.

"I like Tony's explanation a lot better," Alex said. "So, what's next on the schedule?"

"We can drive around," Alfredo said. "And do more rounds of painfully honest toasts, like in a wedding!"

"But who is getting married?" Alex asked, playfully.

"If you'll have me, I'll marry you. Tonight." Alfredo said.

"Sorry, in Philadelphia, we do courtships at a slower pace."

"Alex," Tony said. "If you want to watch a slow pace, watch the teenagers in this park. They might walk around the park for weeks, eyeing each other, before they choose a partner, sit down on a bench and talk. Then they might talk for months before they can hold hands."

"So that's what's going on!" Sarah jumped in. "When we walked through the park, we noticed the groups of boys and girls walking in opposite directions."

Tony explained the tradition of Cuban parks. He must have made it sound very appealing because as soon as he was finished, Alex said:

"We want to try it!"

"Try what?" Alfredo asked, as if he did not know.

"We want to walk around the park, to see what happens," Alex said.

Tony thought that it was a terrible idea, but nothing was stopping these girls. They got out of the car and walked to the park. When they reached the first empty bench, Alex suggested Tony and Alfredo sit there and wait for them to come around again.

"Okay, here we go," Alex said, laughing, as they started on their stroll.

Tony was shocked by this unexpected turn of events. These girls were unpredictable, especially Alex, who seemed to be the leader. But Sarah was no prude. She went along with all of Alex's ideas, and it had been her plan to sneak out with them that night. Tony watched the two girls as they crossed the first group of local boys. The boys looked at them. Sarah and Alex stared back and laughed. After the pass, the local boys broke out talking, excitedly planning their strategy for the next cross.

"How old do you think these girls are?" Tony said. "I think they are older than us."

"Maybe by one year," Alfredo said. "What do you think?"

"Yes, maybe by one year. They sure are crazy. But I like them."

"I like them, too. If they ask, we're fifteen," Alfredo said.

"Okay. We're fifteen. What do we do next?"

"We better get them out of here. When they come back, let's take them to see the turtles."

"Yes, I'm for the turtles," Tony said.

When the girls came around again, they were surrounded by a large group of gregarious and hopeful local boys. Alex said, "Adíos, muchachos," and the two girls rejoined Tony and Alfredo. They were laughing.

"That was fun," Alex said. "We need to start this tradition in Philadelphia parks."

"Can we do it one more time?" Sarah asked. "Then we promise to move on."

So they went around again. It was almost comical. The much anticipated date with the American girls was turning into a disaster.

They returned with a new group of hopefuls. Cuban boys were so predictable, but they only got another *"Adíos muchachos"* for their efforts. As they walked back to the car, Tony told them about the cemetery of the sea turtles. He told them that it was an amazing sight to see, and they might even find a live sea turtle laying eggs.

"I've never been asked on a date to go to a turtle cemetery!" Alex said.

That did not sound like an objection.

"Well, let's go!" Tony said.

They got in the car. Orlando drove through the town, past the entry to Kawama, and then took a right turn onto the coastal road to Matanzas. It was a fifteen-minute drive to the Pines.

The moon was out, and they could see a strong surf pounding on the sandy shore. Alfredo poured another round. He suggested it was Alex's turn to make a painfully honest toast. Alex laughed and said: "A toast to Cuban boys! Especially those who tell us one nice compliment after another, like those boys at the park."

They gulped their drinks down, like cowboys in cowboy movies.

"I hate to tell you," Alfredo said. "But those boys are just trying to pick you up."

"I know, dear, but boys at home never compliment girls. That can be boring."

"Okay, now it's Sarah's turn to toast." Tony said.

"A toast to toasts!"

"Yes," Alfredo said. "To toasts. Fire!"

This is fun, Tony thought. When the summer started, he felt

intimidated by girls, but being on a date with Sarah and Alex seemed easy. The cognac helped. The culture they came from helped. His de la Torre family, for generations, had always looked to America as holding the key to the future, and Tony couldn't agree more. These girls thought that the word chaperone was a strange and out-of-date word associated with Spain and the days of the Conquistadores. Another factor to consider was that Sarah and Alex weren't Catholic, and that had to help. These girls were carefree and natural. And they drank like fish.

Orlando started slowing down, turned off the road and parked under the tall pine trees. He turned toward the back seat and announced: "We're here."

"Another round." Alfredo yelled. "Fire!"

They drank another round and stumbled out of the car. Alfredo led the way through the pine grove. The ocean breeze made an eerie, high pitch sound at the top of the pine trees. An explosion of stars was visible up there. They walked single file with some difficulty because the many toasts were having an effect on everyone. Crashing into a pine tree was a possibility. Everyone was still holding on to the glasses, and Tony was holding on to the bottle. Every now and then, someone stumbled, fell, laughed and got up.

They came out to the open beach. A full moon floated over the water, lighting a surreal landscape of hundreds of evenly spaced sea turtle carcasses. The turtles' shells, measuring up to four-feet across, were mostly intact, as were the head structures. Smaller bones were strewn about each turtle wherever the buzzards had left them.

"This is very spooky," Alex said.

"Don't worry, dear, we're here to protect you," Alfredo said and mimicked a ghostly laugh.

They walked around the carcasses. Tony told Sarah how this

stretch of the beach was both a birthplace and a burial ground for sea turtles; how the ones that were born here roamed the oceans for up to one hundred years and somehow, after all that time, they managed to find this part of the world again at this stretch of beach, and they came here to die.

"That's hard to believe," Sarah said.

"It's true." Tony insisted. "They're like migratory birds. No one understands how they do it."

"It's so sad." Sarah said, looking at a carcass. "That all life, so mysterious and complex, eventually comes down to this, a pile of bones."

"Hey, let's not get too philosophical," Alfredo said. "We'll get depressed, like my idiot brother. Antonio, pass me the bottle. Fire!"

"Dear, you're so prosaic," Alex said.

"Prosaic?" Alfredo hadn't learned that word at Andover.

"Dear, it means—lacking spirituality, which you obviously lack."

"Think of this," Sarah said. "If these turtles lived for a hundred years, they were swimming around during the American Civil War. They saw so much and experienced so much. They learned everything there is to know about life, from the point of view of a turtle. All that history now means nothing. This turtle now is no different from a rock."

"We're reading Sartre," Alex said, laughing. Tony knew that Sartre was one of the authors Julio read.

"Let's toast to Sartre!" Tony said.

"Yes," Alfredo said. "Another drink!"

"I must be morbid, but I also like to go to funerals," Sarah said. "It makes me think about the big picture."

Tony was thinking that Julio would love this girl: she was attractive and fun, read Sartre and thought about the big picture. He also agreed with Sarah; the turtle remains made you think about all the life that turtle lived, and now, what? Someday he, too, would amount to another pile of bones. One minute, he would be alive, full of worries and hopes and plans and then, the next minute, he would be an inert object, no different than a stone. What a depressing thought!

And even more distressing: Sarah, so lovely now, was also going to end up as another pile of bones. But more to the point, here they were: Young and alive and a little drunk on a desolate stretch of beach. He had to try to kiss her.

"Another drink!" Tony yelled.

"Fire! Fire!" Alfredo yelled.

"Boys, boys, calm down," Sarah said. "I think you've reached your alcohol limit. Maybe we should start on our way back. If my parents catch us arriving late, not to mention a little drunk, we'll be grounded, and you will never see us again."

There was a dead silence. All that could be heard was the sound of the surf, and an owl and the wind going through the pines. Tony was shocked. An unexpected curveball and another strike out. There was such a shocking finality to Sarah's statement, and they had been having so much fun.

"Hey, it's still early. The movie isn't over yet!" Alfredo said.

"Sorry boys, but we have to go," Sarah said. She started walking back toward the pine grove.

Even Alex seemed disappointed, but everyone followed, more subdued now. Tony was thinking that Sarah was a strange combination of being wild, like Alex, and being responsible, like at that moment. They made their way back to the car, but not before Alex had picked up a large bone as a souvenir.

"Just the type of item you pick up in the concession stand in a Cuban movie house!" Alfredo said, laughing. That remark lightened the mood, and they all started laughing again.

They stumbled into the back seat. Alfredo told Orlando to take them to the Internacional. Sarah might have felt guilty about cutting the party short because she quickly told Tony that she was glad they came—she had found the turtle cemetery to be strangely moving. Tony quickly pursued the turtle topic. He told her a story how one night he witnessed a giant Kawama laying eggs right in front of his house, and how he had watched the whole operation. The turtle had carefully and with difficulty dug a hole, laid the eggs and then carefully filled the hole with sand. Then she slowly, and sadly, it seemed, returned to the sea. The whole thing took a long time. He had seen Kawamas under water, too, while spear fishing, and in the water they were graceful and fast. But on the sand, moving was a struggle. A few weeks later, early in the morning, he saw the fifteen or twenty tiny baby turtles coming out of their sandy womb, and without hesitation, when they saw the world for the first time, they knew exactly what to do: they made a mad dash for the sea.

No sooner had he finished his story, he noticed—a little shocked—that Alex and Alfredo were kissing. He had not noticed any preliminaries—they had not even engaged in small talk. They sat to their left and went at it. Sarah noticed it, too, and she looked at Tony and smiled.

Tony decided that if he did not try to kiss Sarah now, he would be the world's greatest coward. Still, it was complicated. Was Sarah's little smile an invitation for him to do the same, and kiss her, or was it a smile that said, there goes Alex again, she's a wild girl.

Tony probably looked bewildered, and Sarah must have noticed. She said: "You want to kiss."

Did he want to kiss?

"Yes," he answered, very fast.

Sarah leaned forward and then turned toward Tony. She plant-ed both her arms on either side of him, and slowly moved for-ward, focused on his mouth. Tony took her cue and focused on her mouth. Her mouth came closer, and closer, and their lips touched lightly. Then she started with soft little pecks on his mouth. She kissed him, pulled back and then kissed him again. Then she bored in. Tony tried to follow what she was doing, as if she was leading him on a dance. He knew that he was very lucky to have gone out on a date with Sarah.

He did not know what to do with his arms. They hung by his side, paralyzed. He did not want to do anything foolish and ruin the mood Sarah was in. But after a few minutes of intense kissing, he started thinking that maybe he should be more active with his hands and touch—did he dare think it—a breast!

He raised his hands, and they hovered there, in mid air, while he pondered how to proceed. He started by putting his hands on her waist and drew her toward him. Sarah did not mind. They must have kissed for minutes before Sarah said: "You can touch my breasts, over my dress."

Bingo! Were all American girls like this one? At that moment, he decided: the sooner he went to school in America, the better. At Choate, a thousand American girls would surround him. No more Cuban girls. No more chaperones. Cuban culture was definitely out of touch with modern times.

He must have kissed and touched her breasts over her dress all the way back to the Internacional. The drive took longer than normal because during the middle of the festivities on the back seat, Alfredo had been alert enough to tell Orlando to drive slow-ly. Tony did not remember exchanging one word with Sarah. He never imagined that kissing could be so much fun. He did a lot of experimenting in that first session, thanks to Sarah, who initiated everything, including some explorations with her tongue, which now did not seem disgusting at all.

Throughout it all, he had had an erection, and he hoped that Sarah would not notice. After a while, everything down there had started to hurt, but he ignored it. Kissing Sarah and touching her breasts over her dress was the most exciting thing he had ever done. The dress was light enough so that he could feel the contours of her flesh. His primal instincts must have taken over because he wanted more. He placed his hand on her bare skin, just above her dress, and started to slip it down, but Sarah quickly stopped that. She took his hand and placed it back on top of her dress. Those were the rules, and he did not want to push his luck.

SARAH'S family was in Varadero for one week, and they managed to sneak out with the girls every night. They went to "the movies" a few more times, until Sarah's parents became suspicious and prohibited the girls from leaving the hotel grounds. On one of the movie nights they went to Cardenas, the port town on the underside of the Hicacos Peninsula. They watched the dating rituals in their central square. Alex and Sarah did their walk around the park, but the boys in Cardenas did not get many tourists to come their way, and they must have been intimidated by Alex and Sarah because they did not stick to the girls like glue, like the boys at the square in Varadero. They walked around the port and found an outdoor bar with a jukebox, ordered rum and cokes and danced the cha-cha-chá. After a few drinks, they could almost do it. The last time they used the movies as an excuse they drove to the tip of the Hicacos Peninsula, parked by the water, drank in the back seat and kissed. Then they got out and went on a walk by the surf. They noticed a small but thick black cloud moving toward them. At first, they didn't know what it was, but then the black cloud started biting them. Mosquitos! They had to run back to the car.

They switched drinks, from Cognac to Cointreau because Alfredo had heard that Cointreau was an aphrodisiac. And it must have worked some because Tony's kissing bouts with Sarah continued at a furious pace. He tried a few more times to touch her breasts under the dress, but Sarah grabbed his wandering hand and resolutely said: "No." He asked Alfredo how far he had gone with Alex; she had imposed the same limits on him. Still, Tony and Alfredo weren't complaining.

When the girls got grounded, they met on the beach in front of the hotel after Sarah's parents hit the casino. There was a row of small sailboats up on the sand, and if they sat on the ocean side, shielded by the boats, no one in the hotel could see them. They brought the shot glasses and the Cointreau and used the boats for a backrest.

On the last night, he exchanged addresses with Sarah and made plans to write. Their last kissing session was especially memorable. He tried one more time to slip his hand under the top of her dress, and Sarah did not stop him. He kept his hand there, and Sarah did not say: "No!" That must have been her farewell present.

19

THEN SHE WAS GONE. HE MISSED her, but he also felt a distinct feeling of well-being. An attractive, exciting and older American girl had kissed him during an entire one-week vacation. His life with girls had taken one giant step forward. He missed her, but he didn't feel sad. It wasn't a goodbye. It was more like a see-you-later. He was already planning his next move. He would write to her and make plans to see her again when he went to school in the States. They could meet in New York. He wanted to continue with their kissing marathons, but he also wanted to see her again for other reasons. Sarah was different from any girl he had known. She didn't live by rules or conventions. In Cuba, everyone followed the rules: Catholic rules, society's rules and their parent's rules. Sarah made her own rules.

After they left, Alfredo wanted to go back to the Internacional right away to find more American girls. At first, Tony resisted the idea. It didn't feel right, as if they were being unfaithful to Sarah and Alex, but Alfredo persisted and after a few days, Tony agreed. Alfredo's argument was simple; they had found a gold mine at the Internacional. Why not mine it some more?

Why not, Tony decided. He was not going to forget Sarah—he planned to see her again—but there was more to learn from other American girls. This was all part of being a doer, as Gonzalo had advised.

They skied to the Internacional and thoroughly checked the hotel grounds—the beach area, the swimming pool, the hotel lobby, but when they saw two girls alone, they ran into the same familiar problem—they never seemed to be the right age. They tried again to impress the older girls, but got the same results as before. The girls were amused, but only for a short time. They were perhaps thinking that the sight of two fourteen-year-old boys trying to pick up grown women verged on the ridiculous or the perverted.

One day they watched the old pro, Robertico Arteaga and another boy from the older group. They went to work on two older girls sitting by the pool. When Robertico moved in on them, they perked up and paid attention. Robertico was charming and good-looking, and he was close to their age. Soon they were all laughing and getting along. Then Robertico left the group for a minute and a few moments later returned with a tray of drinks and shrimp appetizers. How thoughtful, Tony thought. He was such a slick mover! Shortly after the appetizers, they headed for the beach and the main course. They climbed onto Robertico's motorboat, and the boat sped eastward, past the DuPont mansion. It was a matter of time before one of those girls levitated and flew into Robertico's arms, like the girl at Marina.

After one week of daily trips to the Internacional and daily rejections, they gave up. It became obvious that what had happened with Sarah and Alex was not going to happen again. Sarah and Alex were unique; they were as interested as boys in making out and drinking, and they did not mind going out with boys one year younger. Tony and Alfredo had been very lucky to meet them. Tony wished he had taken a picture of Sarah with his Brownie. He could still see her in his mind, but she was becoming more out-of-focus with each passing day.

Increasingly, he couldn't help thinking about Sarah whenever he looked westward down the beach and could make out the distant outline of the Pines. He could not look at Alfredo's father's black Cadillac, harmlessly parked in his driveway, without remembering their backseat adventures. Every time they went to the Internacional, everything there reminded Tony of Sarah.

One week after Sarah left, he wrote her a letter. He wanted to tell her that he was thinking about her all the time; that he missed her, and everything in Varadero seemed to remind him of her; that he was thinking about how much he had enjoyed her company and how much he had enjoyed the car trips with her.

Instead, he told her what he was doing. This took some effort because he did not say anything about going back to the Internacional, or the daily tennis game with Carmen. He had trouble ending the letter. He finally decided to keep it simple and say, in a separate line at the end: I miss you. He sent the letter special delivery.

More than one week went by without receiving a letter back. He wondered if he had written a bad letter, a letter that had not said enough, or the opposite, a letter that implied too much with that simple ending; I miss you. Maybe that simple ending had scared her. He didn't know what to think.

ONE morning, while walking down the beach with Alfredo, they waded into the group in front of Enrique Estrada's house. The group's conversation seemed so silly, all about who liked whom in their group, with the accused pair vigorously denying everything. He was relieved, nevertheless, when no one kidded him about Carmen. Their tennis game must have gone unnoticed, even though they had continued playing every day, even while he was going out at night with Sarah.

He knew Carmen was never going to sneak out at night with him, drink Cointreau and neck in the backseat of a car. With Carmen, all he could do was play tennis and talk, but when she talked, she became very animated, and her hair flew around. She was fun to watch as she gossiped, told a story or expressed an opinion, and what she said was interesting. With Carmen, it was okay to overlook her Cuban propriety and just talk to her.

During their daily conversations after the tennis match, Carmen continued to steer the conversation toward politics and how she thought Batista was going to be a disaster for Cuba. For the sake of arguing, Tony took an opposite position. He knew from his Cuban history class that Batista had been an elected president in the forties and had not been a bad president. So now he had taken power illegally, but Tony had heard his father say that there was very little opposition to his 1952 coup because the president he deposed was so corrupt that the public reaction had been to say 'good riddance.' Batista would not turn out any different from elected presidents because everyone agreed that elected presidents all turned into crooks after taking office.

Carmen laughed. "That is a silly argument," she said. "Batista played by the rules in the forties, but now he had obviously changed. He took power illegally. Now he is a dictator, unwilling to play by the rules. Now he will do whatever he pleases."

It was hard to argue with Carmen. For one, she seemed to win all the arguments, but talking about politics was not what Tony had in mind. He would have preferred their conversations to be more personal, more about them, but that wasn't happening. It was obvious to him that the reason he was playing tennis every day with Carmen was that she was a very attractive girl. He was attracted to her, and he hoped that maybe they had a future together as a couple. Somehow, any of that was hard to acknowledge in a conversation. It was off limits. Of course, his cousins Tina and Carlos were also sitting there with them. But even if they weren't, Tony suspected his conversation with Carmen would not change too much.

One day, they had a more interesting conversation after the tennis game. Carmen and Tina were talking about a girl in the older group who had recently got engaged, and that led Carmen to tell a story about how her parents got engaged. They had met at their first dance party when they were fifteen. The first time they danced, they simply stared at each other during the entire song and fell instantly in love. It was one of those physical things because they never said a word. The day after that dance, Carmen's father sent flowers to Carmen's mother, and that was it. They dated through high school and college, and then they got married. They never kissed anyone else. And now, sixteen years after their marriage, they were still in love.

Tony liked that story. It seemed that Carmen's parents were destined for each other. They had been dazzled at first sight, and that dazzle persisted. Still, Tony was thinking that if he had been Carmen's father, he would wonder how it would feel to kiss someone else. Kissing a girl was interesting and sexy. He had enjoyed kissing Isabel, and kissing Sarah had been ten times more exciting. Not to mention touching her breasts. It was almost embarrassing for him to admit it, but now he was thinking about kissing Carmen. It would be the ultimate kiss, to kiss Carmen's perfectly formed lips, and he could be almost certain that he would be the first to kiss those lips.

Tony followed Carmen's story with his parent's story, a funny story he had heard at the family dinner table. He remembered asking his mother if the story was true. She laughed and said: "Yes, something like that happened". It seemed that when his mother was single, she had the reputation of being one of the most beautiful women in Havana. Tony's father, Victor de la Torre, also had a reputation. He was a very good athlete, having excelled at all the varsity sports at Choate, and he was handsome and funny. In Havana, they called the de la Torre brothers the Eaton boys because they had all gone to a well-known American prep school and Yale. They had impeccable educational and family credentials.

When his parents went out on their first date, Tony's mom knew right away that he was the man for her, but Victor was not so sure. When he was a senior at Yale, he dated Tony's mom whenever he returned to Cuba on vacations. But he also dated American girls while he was in New Haven. He was having too much fun being a bachelor and was in no rush to get engaged.

Tony's mother had a different idea. She thought that the timing was right for Victor to propose. He was going to work for his father after graduation, helping him manage one of his sugar mills, so his future was assured. She expected a proposal, but the proposal was not forthcoming. So she took matters into her own hands. Just before Victor graduated from Yale, she made a surprisingly bold move—she spread the news in Havana that Victor had proposed.

After graduation, Victor returned to Cuba. The day after he arrived, he went to the bar at the Havana Yacht Club to have some drinks and play dice. As soon as he entered the bar, Mario de la Torriente, an older man he knew, shook his hand:

"Congratulations," he said.

"Thank you," Victor said.

He assumed Mario was referring to his Yale graduation. A few more people at the bar offered more congratulations. He thanked them, too. Then one of his friends said: "You made a fine choice. She's a beautiful woman." Finally, Victor put two and two together. Wherever he went in Havana, the same thing happened. At first he denied the news of his engagement, but he claimed that no one believed him. Finally, Victor decided that it took a lot less effort to go along with the engagement story than to deny it, and that was how they became engaged.

Carmen loved his parent's story. She thought it was impressive how his mother had taken the initiative and how it must have taken a lot of courage to do what she did. Carmen said it was ridiculous how men were the only ones expected to take the initiative when it came to courting, asking someone to marry them or even asking someone to dance.

Tony was impressed. Carmen always seemed ready to advocate a controversial idea and he agreed with that one. He had liked it every time Sarah had taken the initiative, especially in the backseat of the car. Carmen could take that kind of initiative any day, although the chances of that happening were zero. In any case, the conversation about their parents was more in line with what he had in mind. That conversation was about falling in love. He was interested in that topic. He seemed to have a facility for falling in love.

Whatever was going on, or not going on, with him and Carmen was often on his mind, but he also kept thinking about Sarah. Then finally, a letter from Sarah arrived. He could tell it was not very thick and dreaded opening it. When he did open it, he was disappointed.

It was a short letter, and she did not say anything too personal. She did not say that she missed him. She only said a few things about what she was up to in Philadelphia and then how much she had enjoyed her vacation in Varadero. After that mention, she simply said, thank you for a wonderful time, and that was it. He reread the letter at least ten times. He focused again and again on the word wonderful. Okay, she had a wonderful time. She enjoyed the vacation, but she did not say that she was missing him day and night, that her vacation had been the best ever, that boys in Philadelphia were boring compared to him and all were terrible kissers, and she could not wait to kiss him again.

She only said, "thank you for a wonderful time".

It was something, but he wanted more. He had a very bad feeling about the letter. Maybe she had been too shy, as he had been, to say what was really on her mind. Maybe he should have been more honest in his letter. He decided to write back. But this time, he thought, why not say the truth?

He sat down on the table on the porch and wrote his first love letter. He started by saying that since she had left, he had been thinking about her all the time. He was thinking that he was in love with her. It was embarrassing for him to say that, but there it was. He had enjoyed every minute they had spent together, but especially their last night. He couldn't wait to see her again. He wanted to make an arrangement to meet in New York City, on his way to Choate in September. She could take the train from Philadelphia, and he could meet her under the clock at the Biltmore, next to Grand Central. He remembered Alfredo telling him how that was the favorite meeting place for prep school students in New York City. If she couldn't come to New York City, he could take the train to Philadelphia.

The letter was short, honest and direct. He was nervous about mailing it, but he went to the post office in downtown Varadero and mailed it special-delivery once more. Afterwards, he felt very good about having done it. He was becoming a grown-up man. A man of the world.

The letter turned out to be a disaster. He never heard from Sarah again.

20

JUST AS HIS DISTRESS ABOUT Sarah hit a low point, when it was becoming obvious that she was not going to reply, and he was walking around the beach feeling miserable, something significant happened. Carmen showed up alone for the tennis game. She said that Tina had twisted her ankle water-skiing and could not play. But she still wanted to play, so there she was. Did he want to play singles?

"Sure, I would love to play singles," Tony said.

He suggested they hit the ball and work on their strokes, but Carmen insisted on playing for points. She was very competitive and fought hard for every point to no avail. Throughout the game, he kept thinking that for Carmen to show up alone, ready to play singles, was a bold move. This was an omen; from four to two, from the group to only Carmen and Tony. And Carmen had initiated it.

Maybe she had been inspired by his mother's engagement story, not that Carmen needed inspiration to do things differently. Still, if someone saw them playing tennis alone, word would spread around, and the next time she waded into the group in front of Enrique Estrada's house, someone would surely tease her:

"Carmen, I hear you are in love with Tony de la Torre."

He didn't want to think how she might reply to that question.

Nevertheless, Carmen had shown up alone to play tennis with him. When they sat on the terrace for their after-the-game daily ritual of a coke and conversation, it felt different. It felt like a date. He noticed that there were many other couples sitting on the outdoor tables that day; the annual Varadero Regatta was coming up that weekend.

They sat down on one of the few unoccupied tables. It was strange not having Tina and Luis around. It felt like they were taking a new step forward. It was amazing how such a simple activity, having a coke after a tennis game, could mean so much. This new situation clearly called for a more personal conversation than a conversation about politics. His week with Sarah had noticeably improved his confidence. He was thinking that he ready to be more forward and bold, as opposed to shy and hesitant.

"Carmen, I have a question I would like to ask you."

"Ask it," she said

He was ready to ask a very forward and bold question when he noticed a group of adults coming out of the Kawama bar. There was a couple in the group he thought he recognized, and it took him a few seconds to realize who they were: Carlos and Isabel from the Mambo Club. It looked like Carlos had finally come through for Isabel, but they were going to walk by his table on the way out to their car, and he could picture Isabel saying: "How are you, sweetie? What a coincidence, finding you here."

What would Carmen think? Isabel did not look like a woman from a good family. She looked more like a woman who practiced the world's oldest profession. This was a disaster in the making. He thought fast, grabbed the canister with the tennis balls on the empty chair next to his and quickly ducked under the table.

"Tony, what are you doing?"

"The tennis balls fell out of the canister."

"What?"

"I'm looking for the tennis balls."

Carmen lowered her face under the table. "Tony de la Torre! Are you crazy? Come out right now from under the table."

"I found them," Tony said, holding up one of the balls. He watched as the group of legs passed by. "These are my last tennis balls, and I don't want to lose them." He needed to remain under the table a few more seconds.

"Tony de la Torre, if you don't come out from under the table this very second, I will never speak to you again!"

Tony came out. He could see the backs of Carlos and Isabel as their group walked away.

He sat down again. Disaster averted.

"Okay," Tony said. "Are you ready for the question?"

"I'm ready to find out what that was all about."

"I told you, the tennis balls. Okay. Here is what I have in mind. Let's play a game. This game has only one rule. I get to ask you one question, and you have to answer it 100% honestly. Then you can ask me one question, and I have to answer it 100% honestly. When someone refuses to answer a question, they lose the game. Do you dare to play this game?"

"It depends on the question," she said, smiling.

"No, no. That's the point of the game! You have to agree to answer, regardless of the question."

"Go ahead." She seemed amused.

"Think back to last summer, to the week we spent in Ciego. To the night that was so hot that we could not sleep, and we went for a swim in the river. To the moment when we were lying on the riverbank looking at the stars. Have you ever thought about that night? And if you have, what have you thought?"

"Tony de la Torre! What kind of question is that?"

"It's a very simple question."

"Well, no, I haven't thought about that night."

"You don't remember that night?"

"I barely remember it. I remember it was very hot, and we all went swimming, and there were a lot of mosquitoes!"

"That is all you remember?"

"What else am I supposed to remember?" Carmen said, laughing.

"Okay. I guess you answered my question." He was disappointed.

"You sound disappointed."

"No."

"Okay, my turn! Are you ready?"

"Sure."

"Go back to that same night in Ciego. Have you thought about that night and what have you thought?"

"That's not fair!"

"Why not?"

"That was my question. You have to ask your own question."

"You did not say that! All I heard about the rules of this silly game was that I could ask a question, not what kind of question. Are you afraid to answer my question? Have I won this game already?"

Tony was thinking that Carmen was very smart and very tricky, but he was not going to back off. It was his new way of doing things.

"Okay. Have I thought about that night? Yes, I've thought about it. It was a very hot and clear night. We went swimming and afterwards we were lying on our backs. Tina, Luis, you and I. We were staring at the stars. You were lying next to me. We could see the Milky Way very clearly. We talked about the universe and you and I agreed that there had to be millions of stars with planets exactly like Earth, and there was probably life on many of those planets."

"Is that all?" Now it was Carmen who sounded disappointed.

"No."

"Oh, oh."

"Why oh, oh."

"Because I don't think I want to hear the rest."

"Why not?"

"Because you're a boy, and we all know what boys are constantly thinking about."

"What do you think we are constantly thinking about?"

"You know!"

" I don't know."

"Yes, you do," Carmen said, laughing.

"I won the game, then," Tony said, but as soon as he said it, he felt he needed to keep the conversation going in a good direction. He needed to say something nice.

"I enjoyed playing singles with you."

Carmen seemed to soften.

"I did, too," she said.

"We play well together," Tony said. He was thinking well beyond the game of tennis. The game of life.

"Yes, we do, but I could play better. I'll beat you yet. Are you going to Lydia Espino's party on Saturday night?"

"Yes."

"Good. I'll see you there," Carmen said, smiling again.

ON the bicycle ride home, Tony went over every line in the conversation. He liked how it had ended. When she agreed that they played well together, she also had to be thinking, like him, beyond tennis. He also liked how she said she expected to see him at the party, the first dance party for his age group. She obviously expected him to dance with her. And the game they played on the terrace, about telling the truth—that was fun. Carmen had been immediately willing to play, although she chickened out at the end. He still should have gone ahead and told her how, for one year, he had been thinking about how nice it had been to lie side by side, looking at the stars, with their bodies touching, just so slightly.

But then, if he had mentioned anything related to their thighs touching, Carmen would have been horrified. There are limits as to what could be said, even though she probably thought about that moment too and that was why she did not want to hear anything more about it. Was he imagining all this? Maybe she really hadn't thought much about that night, as she claimed. Besides, the memory that there had been a lot of mosquitoes, which was true, because they had run back to the house later that evening.

Now Tony had to move on to his next worry. It was almost as if he had a fixed quota of worries. As soon as some worries receded, new worries replaced them. He was going to his first dance party, and Carmen expected him to dance with her. He barely knew how to dance.

21

TONY AND ALFREDO WERE WALKING
on the bicycle path next to the lagoon, headed for Lydia Espino's
house. Tony was in no rush to get there. His age group had managed to go through most of the summer without a dance party, but
after this one, the floodgates were going to open. A few more were
already scheduled, and he had heard that Enrique Estrada was going to give a dance party and invite Jorge Batista, the dictator's son.
Carmen would die before she went to that party.

Halfway to Lydia's house they passed a group of servants sitting
on Enrique Estrada's lagoon dock. Cairo, the Estrada's chauffeur,
was playing the guitar and singing *La Noche de Anoche*, Yesterday's Night. They stopped walking and listened. Cairo played the
guitar well and sang with a beautiful high-pitched voice:

Yesterday's night.
That was some night, last night.
So many things happened, so suddenly.
They confused me so.

He thought about his first date with Sarah on the night of the turtles. So many things happened. But unlike the song Cairo was singing, Tony had not been confused at all. He had loved every minute of it. At that moment, though, he didn't want to think about Sarah. He was thinking about the inevitable, upcoming dance with Carmen. It could turn into a disaster.

He had worked at improving his dancing skills. Tony's dad watched him on the porch as he tried to learn some dance steps with his sister Sofi. His dad explained to him the hopelessness of his situation. He claimed that in the last three generations of de la Torres, not one de la Torre had known how to dance.

Tony thought that there had to be some truth to that observation. It seemed that the dancing problem was firmly embedded in the de la Torres' genes, but he pointed out to his father that his sister Sofi was a de la Torre, and she was a good dancer. Sure, his father said. The women in the family could dance. The problem was with the men.

Then his dad did something nice. He asked Tony what he was wearing to the dance. Tony was not sure. In a rare act, his dad handed Tony a lot of money. Then he said, "Get a linen guayabera. You can't go wrong with a linen guayabera. Tony took the money, and the next day he bought the guayabera, the long-sleeved white shirt Cubans wore to formal occasions. Later, when he looked at himself in the mirror wearing the guayabera, rather than admiring how well he looked, he felt touched by his father's gesture.

Tony's dance lessons with his sister had not gone well. His sister kept telling him to move to the beat, but apparently, he could not hear the beat, and his memory did not seem to work when it came to remembering dance steps. He was incapable of doing the cha-cha-chá correctly, even though his sister kept telling him that the steps were easy. Some dances he could do. The slow ones, like the *boleros*, but the Mambo and the cha-cha-chá he would have to avoid.

Cairo finished his song, and Tony and Alfredo started walking again. A light breeze was blowing in from the ocean, rustling the fronds of the coconut trees. On the ocean side of the houses, they could hear the muted sounds of waves crashing on the sand, pulling back, then crashing again. Tony loved nights on this beach. Days, too. He liked living in the tropics, close to the water. If there was a god, and this god had designed the human body, he had designed it for this exact spot.

"Antonio," Alfredo said, laughing. "I hear you're looking forward to dancing with Virginia Blanco." Tony laughed softly at Alfredo's cruel joke. Virginia Blanco was pathologically thin and ridiculously flat chested. No one was going to dance with her, except possibly her brother. The only girl he wanted to dance with was Carmen. He wanted to make a statement by asking her to dance—that he was interested in her as a partner, not only in tennis and during the day, but at parties, during the night.

The front door to Lydia's house was open. They walked through an empty living room and arrived at the covered porch facing the ocean. The adults were there, drinks in hand, talking loudly and laughing often. Tony and Alfredo shook hands with the men and lightly kissed the women's cheeks, then went down a few steps to a tiled terrace. This was the arena—the dance floor. Tony was glad to see that a trio was playing. A trio tended to play the slower and more romantic songs.

The boys had staked out one end of the terrace. Tony and Alfredo joined them. On the opposite end stood a group of girls. Tony glanced at the girls and yes—Carmen was there. She was wearing a classic black dress with a low neckline, which fully emphasized the fact that she had broad shoulders and blossoming breasts. It seemed to him that she stood out from the other girls.

The boys were working hard at ignoring the girls on the dance floor, not to mention the girls' mothers on the porch. Tony could tell that the mothers were clearly looking forward to the show that was about to start—the opening act of a mating ritual, which the mothers hoped would conclude, in the not too distant future, at the altar. Getting married to a boy from a good family and having many children—that was every mother's plan for their daughters.

"I think we're supposed to do something," one of the boys said.

"What we're supposed to do is dance with the girls, not stand here like idiots." Alfredo said.

"I'll ask someone to dance when they start the next song," Enrique Estrada said.

Enrique Estrada made Tony feel inadequate. Enrique did everything well. Enrique was one of those boys that did not seem to have a flaw. He was reputed to be a very good dancer. He had impeccable manners. He was tall and good-looking. He remembered jokes. His beachfront was where everyone in Tony's age group congregated, and his father owned a bank. All the girls in Kawama could envision a wonderful future with Enrique.

The trio started playing a popular song, *Angustia*. Bienvenido Granda sang it on the radio. Everyone loved this song. It was poetic and sad. Best of all, it was slow. Tony felt confident he could dance to *Angustia*, with its slow, languid beat. He would take one little step and stop, then another little step and stop. The song had wonderful lyrics:

Anguish, because you are not mine
Torment, because I don't have your love
Anguish, because I won't kiss you again.
Nostalgia, because I won't hear your voice

I won't be able to forget
The nights we spent by the sea
I lost all my illusions when I lost you
And anguish filled my heart

Angustia got the boys moving. Enrique Estrada was the first to venture out, and other boys followed his lead. Very quickly, the dance floor started to fill with couples. Tony looked to see which girls were left. Carmen was already dancing. His suspicion that Carmen would start attracting the attention of the other boys was being confirmed, and now he was more determined than ever to dance with her, and fast.

He noticed how gracefully Enrique Estrada danced, and the girl he was dancing with looked as if she were in heaven. He felt sorry for Virginia Blanco, the girl without breasts, sitting by herself at the edge of the dance floor. But not so sorry that he felt the need to ask her to dance.

Alfredo was dancing with Eugenia Sanchez, the girl he liked. They were made for each other because Alfredo was close to six feet tall, and Eugenia was the tallest girl in their group. They danced well together, and every time Alfredo said something, Eugenia laughed. Alfredo could make girls laugh. He wondered what Alfredo was saying that had Eugenia so amused.

The song ended. The dancers dispersed and headed back to their original groups. Carmen was alone again. Tony thought: do it, do it. Don't be a coward.

He walked over. As he made his way through the dance floor, he wondered if Carmen knew that he was a terrible dancer. Maybe his sister had told her friends, and someone had told Carmen. What if Carmen said no? Not likely. But what if she said yes and they played a fast song? How embarrassing! Maybe he should wait until he heard the song. Then, if it was slow, ask Carmen to dance. But he would run the risk that her new admirers would ask her first. Maybe he should stop thinking and just do it—ask her to dance. By the time he was in front of her, his mouth felt dry. He could barely form the words:

"Carmen, do…you…want to dance?"

"Yes," she said, smiling.

He felt an overwhelming sense of relief and gratitude. Not only had she said yes, but she also had said it quickly.

They moved to the dance floor as the trio struck the new song. Thank God, Tony thought. Another slow song. *Miénteme*. Lie to Me. The song was perfect—slow and romantic. Olga Guillot, a very sexy singer, had recently made it a hit. It had some good lines:

> *I know you lie to me.*
> *I know your love is not sincere.*
> *I know you lie when you kiss me*
> *And you lie when you say you love me.*
>
> *I accept it.*
> *Lie to me all you want*
> *Lie to me for an eternity.*
> *Your wickedness makes me happy.*

Tony was thinking how much he was already lying to Carmen, by not telling her about Sarah or about his misadventures at the brothels. But technically, he had never lied to her because she had never asked him about his other life. Also, he was being more honest with her every day. He was letting her know, in small ways, that he liked her. Being honest was an important goal for his new and bolder personality.

Now he was thinking how delightful it would be if Carmen danced closer than the couples he had watched during the first dance. He could try to get Carmen to dance closer by applying a small amount of pressure with his right arm, drawing her towards him, but this would only be met by an equal and opposite force. Newtonian physics, Cuban style. They started dancing. As he expected, Carmen kept her distance.

Tony was thinking that the one good thing about dancing at a distance was that he could stare at his partner. Carmen looked so good that he suspected he did not deserve her. The first thing one noticed about Carmen was her impressive mane of black hair and her gray-brown eyes. Then, her perfectly formed lips. There was always a little smile forming on those lips. Her smile was charming, as if she were about to commit a naughty crime. He couldn't fault anything about her figure. He was convinced there was a rule in nature that mated attractive girls to attractive boys. She was out of his league, as far as looks were concerned.

His immediate problem, though, was the fact that they had danced for a while and not talked. It was interesting how they stared at each other and smiled, but now it was time to say something. Something witty.

"I bet I know what those chaperones on the porch are thinking," he said.

"What?"

"That poor boy, he's a de la Torre, and he's attempting to dance," he said, mimicking the voice of an elderly lady.

Carmen laughed.

"Why are there so many chaperones?" Tony continued, encouraged. "I would not mind if there were one or two, but why twenty?"

"Tony, the chaperones are here because Cuban boys have a record of being untrustworthy."

"Carmen, don't you trust me?"

"I don't know. Should I trust you?"

"No."

"See! That's why we have chaperones."

"Carmen, chaperones are a very bad idea. The adults are saying that you and I can't think for ourselves and we can't make our own decisions. It's an antiquated custom. Developed nations, like the United States, don't believe in chaperones."

"Yes, but in the United States, they don't have Cuban boys."

Tony laughed. "Carmen, if your mother was here, do you think she would be happy or disappointed seeing you dancing with me?"

"I bet she would be delighted," Carmen said.

Carmen was right. Tony knew that his family's name was an old and respectable name in Havana society. On the other hand, Carmen's mother was an intellectual, and there were no artists or writers or intellectuals in the de la Torre family. Historically, all the men in his family had been businessmen. He had always assumed that he would also be a businessman, but he could become interested in doing something else. Who could possibly want to spend their professional life selling refrigerators?

"Carmen, since you seem to think that your mother would be delighted to see us dancing together, maybe she wouldn't mind if we danced closer."

"Tony, are you a pervert!" Carmen said, more amused than shocked.

"Boys are perverse," Tony said.

"Speak for yourself. I know some boys who aren't."

"Who?"

"Enrique Estrada is very polite."

Oh, God, he shouldn't have asked. He was hoping Carmen had no interest in the Perfect Boy. If he had to compete with Enrique, he knew he would be in serious trouble. When the song ended, he thought about a more pressing problem. After two slow songs, the trio was likely to strike up something fast. Sure enough, they did. They played *La Enganadora*, The Deceiver, a very lively cha-cha-chá about a woman notorious for her large breasts, which were discovered to be false. He had to move fast.

"I'm starving," Tony said. "Do you want to get something to eat?"

She claimed she was hungry, too. She probably suspected his dancing limitations and was being nice. They went up to the porch and made their way to the dining room, served themselves some *paella* and returned outside. They found an empty table next to the low wall that marked the edge of the terrace. Beyond were thirty yards of sand, then the ocean.

"So," Carmen said, smiling mischievously. "What else do perverse boys think about?"

What a question! He had to seize the moment.

"Carmen, if you really want to know, perverse boys always tell the truth."

"Are we playing that silly game again?"

"Yes. I think you look stunning tonight."

For one brief moment, Carmen looked surprised. But then she said:

"Thank you. That's very nice of you. Do you say this to every girl?"

"No."

It was true. This was the first time. And he meant it. Now that he had said it, he felt good, and the compliment seemed to work.

Carmen looked pleased. He was on a roll now, trying to come up with another bold yet truthful compliment.

"I like your dress," Tony said. "It's very elegant."

"Thank you," she said, and this time she didn't add anything else.

He was considering following that with: "I really like you," but decided against it. That would be going too far, even though it was obvious. He was thinking about what else he could say when he saw that Alfredo and Eugenia Sanchez, plates in their hands, were walking toward their table.

"Carmen," Alfredo said, laughing. "What bad luck! Of all the boys in this party, you end up with Antonio!"

"I have no complaints," Carmen said.

What a terrific answer, Tony thought.

Alfredo and Eugenia sat down. They all ate the paella, which was delicious, and watched the dancers. As soon as they finished eating, Tony could not wait to dance again. After his skillfully delivered compliments and her "no complaints" statement, he was thinking that their relationship was ready for a new stage.

He was about to ask her to dance when a group of boys and girls passed by their table, sat on the concrete wall and lowered themselves down to the sand. They started walking toward a group by the surf.

"What's going on?" Tony asked.

"The de Silva brothers are fighting again."

Before the summer started, Tony had seen the de Silva brothers sparring against each other in the gym at the Havana Yacht Club. They were skilled boxers and seemed to enjoy hitting each other.

"What are they fighting about?" Alfredo asked.

"José called Jorge an *hijo de prostituta*." That was the polite way of saying it.

Even Carmen and Eugenia laughed. Everyone knew that the de Silva brothers were crazy.

"Let's go watch the stupid jerks," Alfredo said.

Tony was thinking that if they went down to the sand to watch the fight, they would temporarily get away from the chaperones. This little plot was worth pursuing.

"Let's go watch," Tony said, getting up.

Carmen and Eugenia did not object, Tony thought, because half the party seemed to be moving toward the commotion on the sand. When they got there, the brothers were circling each other, their guards up, boxing style. They were throwing jabs and an occasional right, but the punches were missing. Then one of the brothers charged and connected with a flurry of vicious short, sharp hooks to the body, to the face. The other brother immediately retaliated with a similar outburst of punches. When they moved apart, with their fists raised again, one of the brothers had blood running down his nose. Friends stepped in, and the fight was over.

The crowd started to move back toward Lydia's house, but a few couples continued walking toward the surf. Alfredo and Eugenia had already started walking back.

"Let's walk by the water," Tony said.

"I don't know. Should I trust you without the chaperones watching us?" Carmen said, but she was smiling.

"Come on, Carmen. You know the saying: A dog that barks doesn't bite."

"I don't believe that saying. Some dogs that bark also bite."

Still, they started walking toward the surf. Tony could not believe how easy it had been to move away from the house and the chaperones. Now that it had been established, in his mind, that Carmen liked him, was she challenging him to do something?

The breeze had quieted down. Close to the water, Tony could

see that the ocean was calm. He picked up a stone from the sand. "Look, Carmen," he said, as he threw the stone in the ocean. The splash glowed. The water was phosphorescent. This happened for a few weeks every summer, when the water temperature was just right and the tiny living organisms that glowed flourished. They continued walking. Carmen was wearing short heels, which was making walking on the sand difficult. She bent down, holding on to Tony, and removed one shoe, then the other.

He liked how she had leaned on him. How she touched him and depended on his support to hold her balance. It was his turn to do something. What was he supposed to do—kiss her? Everyone knew that well-brought-up Cuban girls did not kiss.

Still, this situation was a gift from fate, luck or the crazy de Silva brothers, and he should try to kiss her. And if he tried to kiss her, should he ask her or should he simply do it? Sarah asked him, and he was very glad she did. He knew that if there was a perfect moment, this was it. It was dark by the water. No one back in the house would be able to see them. If he did not try to kiss her, he would never forgive himself. They were walking close together, moving away from the Espino's house. For starters, he would put his arm around her waist. If she did not mind that move, then he would ask her.

Tony's arm moved up behind her back, hovered there in mid-air and then docked around her waist.

"Tony, what are you doing?"

He quickly removed his arm, as if he had touched a hot pan.

"I think we better get back," she said, but without much conviction. She continued walking in the same direction. This was all the encouragement Tony needed.

"Carmen, I was thinking that this is your best chance to kiss a boy."

Carmen laughed loudly. She stopped walking and faced him. "Tony, are you nuts? Are you asking me if you can kiss me?"

Christ, this is embarrassing, Tony thought.

"Yes," he said.

"Well, the answer is no."

They started walking again. The direction was still favorable.

"Just a little kiss," he said. "No one can see us."

"No. Is this all you think about?"

"I guess so."

She looked at him and laughed. They continued walking.

"We should go back," she said.

Did he detect a conspiratorial tone? Was being found out her only worry?

"Carmen," he pleaded. "Just…one…tiny…little…kiss."

She stopped walking, looked around, faced him and smiled: "All right. You are very persistent. You can kiss me on my cheek."

Bingo! But on her cheek? Not what he had in mind. She turned her face slightly and closed her eyes.

He did not want the kiss to be a fleeting, perfunctory kiss—the way he kissed his aunts—so he moved in slowly, focused on the approaching, tanned cheek, and increasingly on the corner of her lips. He aimed the kiss so a good portion of his lips, maybe as much as half, touched hers. Once he made contact, he lingered there, glued. Then something amazing happened. Carmen moved her lips to fully meet his. Seconds passed, then she moved her face away.

"Let's go back now," she said.

They started walking back toward the house. Tony was stunned. Did he do that? Did she do that? He did not say anything, not wanting to ruin the mood by saying something trivial or stupid. He knew something important had happened. He kissed Carmen, and she kissed him back! She truly had to like him to kiss him. Did this mean that Carmen was his girlfriend?

They returned to the terrace and sat down at their table as the trio started playing *La Noche de Anoche*, the song Cairo had been singing on the lagoon dock. It was an omen. He knew that this song was going to be their song. They listened to the first lines:

> *That was some night, last night,*
> *So many things happened, so suddenly.*
> *They confused me so.*
> *I'm stunned.*
> *Me, who had been feeling so peaceful.*
> *Yesterday's night*
> *What a marvelous revelation.*
> *I now understand that I've lived all my life waiting*
>   *for you.*

That was exactly how he felt. He stood up and asked Carmen to dance, offering his hand to her, to the first Cuban girl from his group he had kissed, to his first true love. When she said yes, he heard a yes to their future, to a life together. And when they danced, Carmen danced much closer. He was lost in the words of the song, identifying with the singer, stunned like him by the events of the night, thinking that the girl in his arms was beautiful, and she loved him. He felt a blissful feeling envelop him. A feeling he had never felt before.

Even his dancing at that moment was masterful.

22

WHEN TONY WOKE UP EARLY ON
Sunday morning, the morning after he kissed Carmen, he felt like
those people in voodoo movies that go into a trance after drinking
a secret potion. He had drunk from the cup of love, and he was
feeling the after effects—the blissful, dizzy feeling that enveloped
him while he danced with Carmen to *La Noche de Anoche*.

The blissful feeling was still there that morning and throughout
the day. He felt it during the entire week. That week, he thought,
was one of the best weeks of his life. He didn't have one single
negative thought. He felt like a different person, overflowing with
charm and confidence.

He was in love, and the girl he was in love with, as far as he was
concerned, was the most beautiful and wittiest girl on the beach.
And best of all, she was his girl. He was sure about that because

Carmen kissed him and danced closer than normal. That could only be interpreted as her declaration that she loved him, too. The kiss on the sand turned out to be a magical kiss—it seemed to have changed his demeanor and his personality. It was amazing. The power of love.

When he got up that Sunday morning, like a true zombie, he felt a strange compulsion to get on his bicycle and ride over to Tina's house. It was still dark, although he could see a glow on the eastern sky. There was no one about, not even a cat. He left the bicycle on the road in front of Tina's house and made his way into the garden. Tina's mother believed that gardens in the tropics should mimic dense tropical jungles, and she more than succeeded with her Varadero garden.

Tony crawled like a thief into the dense vegetation until he found himself right under Tina and Carmen's second-floor bedroom. He found a good spot under giant ferns with a good view of their window. He sat on the ground and didn't move for a while.

He closed his eyes and imagined the scene in the bedroom. Carmen slept like an angel, covered by a white linen sheet, dreaming a pleasant dream because he imagined her smiling while she slept. She could be dreaming about him. She could be dreaming about the kiss.

His meditation was interrupted by the mosquitoes, which started biting. The mosquito bites didn't bother him. He was in a trance. Still, the mosquitoes kept biting. It was annoying. His instinct was to slap them hard and kill them, but he had to do it without making loud slapping noises. He had to muffle the slaps. It would be a disaster if someone discovered him hiding under the bushes in Tina's garden at six in the morning. Then he started feeling another kind of pain, a much more intense pain, coming from his feet and legs. *Ay Coñooooooooo!* He must have sat on top of a fire ant hill. *Hormigas bravas*, mad ants, as Cubans called them, and they were mad at him. Tony started jumping up and down. Finally, he ran out of there fast. Back on the road, he brushed off all the ants still crawling on his feet and legs, jumped on his bike and rode home.

Later that morning he walked to Tina's house. He walked down the beach, aware of his excellent new mood, sporting a newly acquired permanent smile. He said hello to everyone he passed. He felt more sociable than he would normally feel. He greeted a group of men smoking cigars in the water, waded in and shook hands with all of them. He had to work at being friendlier with his father's friends because they could undoubtedly help him in business if he decided to be a businessman. He had to get serious about his future. His future could include Carmen, and she deserved to marry a wealthy man.

He passed Enrique Estrada's group and again, he waded into the water and shook hands with the boys and kissed all the girls. The boys in Enrique Estrada's group did not seem too intimidating that day. After all, Carmen had chosen to kiss him, not them. He joined in the group's silly conversation for a while and then continued on his way to Tina's house.

Carmen and Tina were in the water, talking to the two boys who lived next door. He noticed how Carmen seemed happy to see him and how she smiled at him with a knowing smile. It was not a standard smile—it had a touch of naughtiness—as if she were saying: I enjoyed what we did last night!

Tony smiled back with his newly acquired permanent smile. He thought he modified it, so as to say: yes, I know what we did last night, and I also enjoyed it.

He didn't have any problems talking to Carmen. He didn't worry about what to say. Their conversation was relaxed, and it flowed easily. They talked about trivial things, and what had happened between them during the party was not alluded to in any way, except possibly with their smiles. But Tony could tell Carmen was acting differently toward him. She was very focused on him. She ignored the other two boys after he arrived.

Tony asked her if she wanted to go for a walk down the beach. Maybe they could drop by the Estrada's group. Sure, Carmen said. Tina came, too. The moment they started walking, Tony realized that the walk could prove to be an enormous test, and a declaration for all to see, that they were a couple. All he had to do was hold hands with Carmen as they walked. He had no idea if they were at the holding hands stage, but he was willing to find out. He positioned himself next to Carmen, his right hand dangling close to Carmen's left hand.

Their arms swung freely for a while. Every now and then, one of them picked up a shell, showed it to others and dropped it back on the sand. Then, during a lull of shell picking, he made his move. Like a moray eel darting out of her den to snatch an unsuspecting sardine, his hand darted out and held on to Carmen's hand. He could tell by the way she looked at him that she was surprised, but she allowed him to hold on. They held hands for a good thirty yards. As they approached Enrique Estrada's house, she let go, picked up a shell and made no moves to hold hands again. Clearly, she still wasn't comfortable holding hands in front of that group, but it had been an excellent start.

The walk on the beach set the tone for the rest of the week. He was feeling so good about what was happening with Carmen that he became a noticeably better person. He paid more attention to his younger siblings, whom he usually ignored. They were four, five and eight years younger than he was. They had few interests in common, but when he returned to his house, he built a huge sandcastle with them. At lunch, he made it a point to engage in conversations with the adults. He asked them about their morning activities. He even asked his father for his opinion, something he rarely did—whether he should study engineering in college, as his father had, or business. Everyone at the table seemed surprised by his question, not only because he was just fourteen and hadn't even started high school, but also because he had interrupted an argument among the men about the best way to cook a whole pig. His father chuckled and replied with a thoughtful answer. Engineers made things, he said, and businessmen sold them. And the money was always in sales. That sounded like excellent advice.

His week with Carmen went exceedingly well. On Monday, they held hands again as they walked down the beach, but this time for about one hundred yards. On Tuesday, they made it official— that they were a couple. As they approached Enrique Estrada's group, Carmen didn't let go of his hand. Tony was as surprised as everyone in the water. When Tony looked in their direction, the entire group was staring at them. Within hours, everyone on the beach would hear about it.

After holding hands had been established as the norm, Tony started to think about kissing her again. The first kiss had been a special kiss, a magical kiss because it had changed their relationship as well as his demeanor and personality. A second kiss would improve his demeanor and personality even more. He was also thinking that the first kiss had not been an honest kiss. It was supposed to be a kiss on the cheek, but he had aimed for the corner of her lips, and then Carmen had maneuvered it into something more. Now he was interested in a more direct, more honest and more intense kiss, like a kiss between the leading actors in a movie. He had always been attracted to Carmen's perfectly formed lips. If he kissed those lips again, he wanted to be more deliberate about it. It could happen because Carmen was unconventional and she was going along with holding hands. Kissing again seemed like the logical next step.

But kissing Carmen again presented a difficult challenge. There seemed to be very clear rules about what was proper in a Cuban courtship—nothing was allowed beyond holding hands until after the wedding ceremony. To enforce this courtship etiquette, the adults had a clear strategy: never leave a couple alone. Tony did play tennis alone with Carmen at Club Kawama, and they drank cokes on the terrace afterward, but it was a public place, in plain daylight, and family friends were always passing by their table on their way to the bar. If he kissed her again, it had to happen at night, in a place where no one could see them.

There was another dance party coming up on Saturday. Maybe he could get lucky again and manage to escape the party to find himself alone with Carmen. Maybe the de Silvas brothers would get into another fight, but that was a long shot.

His inability to come up with a realistic plan to kiss Carmen again did not spoil his upbeat mood. He was enjoying his new self-image as a man of the world, a man with an attractive girlfriend, a man with an ongoing romance. A true romance, like the one he was experiencing, could thrive on a more spiritual, more platonic level. A true romance seemed to transcend sex.

THE highpoint of the week came on Friday. Earlier that week Tony confessed to Alfredo that something was starting to happen between him and Carmen. Alfredo suggested that they go out on a double date. Alfredo would invite Eugenia, and they could go out for dinner and dancing at Club Kawama. It would be their first official dates with girls in their group. They would also have to line up a chaperone. Tía Nina heard about the plan from Tina and volunteered. She and Tío Carlos would come and have drinks at the bar. Tía Nina then told Tony's parents and insisted they show up, too. After all, watching their son's first official date was not an event to be missed.

Tony called Club Kawama and reserved a table for four on the terrace. It would be too noisy and unromantic at the tables inside the bar, not to mention that his parents and the official chaperone would be there. Rain could spoil the plan, but it turned out to be a clear night.

Tony and Alfredo arrived at Club Kawama first. The waiter brought some special candles to keep the mosquitoes at bay. A trio was playing *boleros* in the bar, and they could hear the music at just the right volume. Carmen, Eugenia and his aunt and uncle arrived together. After a round of handshakes and kissing, the girls sat down, and the adults went inside to the bar. Tony's parents arrived shortly afterward. Another round of handshakes and kissing and his parents also headed for the bar.

Carmen was wearing a red strapless chiffon dress that fit her perfectly. Her bountiful mane of hair had been done up very nicely by a hairdresser. She looked older and more sophisticated than a thirteen-year-old girl. When boys passed by their table on the way to the bar, Tony noticed how they seemed to focus on Carmen, especially the boys from the older group who gravitated to the Club Kawama bar on Friday nights. He could tell that the older boys were wondering about the girl in the red dress and how come they hadn't noticed her before. They had not paid too much attention to any of the girls in the younger group, but they were paying attention now. One group of older boys passed by their table. Before they entered the bar, they stopped and turned to look at them. The boy they called Yeye said something funny, and all his friends laughed. They were probably amazed how fast time passes, and how the younger group was already going out on dates at Club Kawama. Yeye might have commented, when they all laughed, that the de la Torre boy was way over his head. Still, the attention that Carmen was getting from the older boys didn't threaten Tony. Just the opposite. It made him feel good. She was his date.

The evening was a success. He managed to come out with some funny statements that made everyone at their table laugh. Carmen was also funny, and the few times the conversation turned serious, she more than held her own. Even Alfredo, an accomplished cynic, seemed impressed by Carmen. Best of all, Tony thought, Carmen paid attention to him when he spoke. She agreed with him when he offered an opinion, and he noticed how she leaned toward him after dinner and seemed to want to talk with him more than with Alfredo or Eugenia.

Then they all went inside the bar to dance. That moment was a perfect moment. The bar was noisy, smoky and more crowded than usual. His parents, his aunt and uncle were seated at a table, drinking highballs, all smiling, staring at them. There was also a large group of loud and jovial older boys, all in various stages of inebriation. Some were staring at Carmen. He was nervous, but Carmen didn't seem to be nervous or distracted by the complicated social situation inside the bar. She ignored everyone. She seemed intensely focused on Tony. She really seemed to enjoy dancing with him. She made him feel that he was a great dancer. She made him feel that, out of all the boys in the bar, he was the only boy she wanted to be with.

When Tony returned home that night, he went to the porch and sat on a rocking chair facing the moonlit ocean. It felt good to sit there, taking in the salty breeze, the sounds of the surf and the scent of night-blooming jasmine. He could not imagine how he was going to enjoy living in Wallingford, Connecticut, with freezing temperatures, with trees without leaves and no Caribbean ocean. On the other hand, he could count on always coming back to this beach, for every summer vacation, for the rest of his life.

He sat there for a long while, knowing that he wouldn't be able to go to his room and fall asleep. He thought about all the good things that happened during his first official date with Carmen. It had been the best night of his life. Even if nothing more ever happened with Carmen, and in the future they went their separate ways, he would never forget that she was his first real love. He would never forget how good it felt to be in love. It was the best feeling in the world. Nothing could ever match it.

THE feeling of being in love lasted for one day.

The problems started the next night, at the second dance party. A group of boys from the older group crashed the party. They stood there at the edge of the dance floor, like predators, ready to pounce. Then they all moved in and started dancing with the girls. The girls in his group were delighted. The older boys were full-grown men. They were more sophisticated, they were better dancers, and they had cars. It was going to be hard to compete with them.

One of them cut in when Tony was dancing with Carmen. From that moment on, Carmen was in high demand as a dance partner during the last parties of the summer. Tony kept dancing with Carmen, but he had to work hard to get a chance to dance with her. Even when he danced with her, the older boys kept cutting in. What was worse, Carmen seemed pleased that the older boys wanted to dance with her. Tony had to admit that those boys were good dancers. Some were also good looking, and some were very funny.

In a way, it was his fault. He had discovered Carmen. She was a rare diamond, and he had unearthed her. When he took her to Club Kawama, it was like her unofficial debutante party. The older boys got a good look at her, and now all of them were after her. The older boys were very tough competition, unlike the two idiot boys his age who lived next to Tina's house.

Tony could understand what was happening from Carmen's point of view. All along, he thought she was more mature and sophisticated than he was. She was very young, starting her social career. It would be silly for her to get too attached to the first boy that had paid attention to her. She was beautiful, witty, smart and had a promising social future ahead of her.

Then, during the last dance party of the summer, disaster struck. Robertico Artiaga, the boy who made girls levitate, cut in when Tony was dancing with Carmen. What could he do? Tell him no, he couldn't cut in because he had witnessed his depraved life at the brothels? It was pure torture, to watch Carmen dance with him and laugh at everything Robertico said.

Robertico stood out on the dance floor. Self-assured, tall and handsome. And he danced well, too. He kept dancing with Carmen and wouldn't let go. When another older boy tried to cut in, Robertico simply said: no, sorry, she's with me, and Carmen didn't protest. She seemed so amused by him, much more amused than when Tony danced with her. Tony felt miserable that night and humiliated because Carmen seemed to have forgotten that he existed. While she danced with Robertico, she was very focused on him. She didn't even look once in Tony's direction.

He couldn't watch them any longer. He left the party and walked home. He felt miserable that night, and he felt even worse the few days after that party as he continued to stew on his misery. Then, almost in unison, everyone in Varadero Beach boarded the windows of their houses and moved back to Havana.

The car trip back to Havana was always depressing because it marked the end of the summer. But this time, Tony felt doubly depressed. He was riding in the front next to Gonzalo, on Gonzalo's second trip back to Havana, with the car loaded with suitcases. Gonzalo was typically talkative, carrying on about how he couldn't wait to get back to Havana to service his harem, but Tony didn't want to talk. He certainly didn't want to talk about Gonzalo's sex life. He couldn't understand how his wonderful week with Carmen, and their perfect night at Club Kawama, had come to such a disastrous conclusion during the last dance party of the summer. It was beyond comprehension. It had never occurred to him that all the romantic feelings he had been feeling toward Carmen were not exactly reciprocated. Even if those feelings had been reciprocated, especially during the night at Club Kawama, they had been extremely short-lived. How was that possible?

He only saw her once in Havana before he left for Choate. They talked briefly after Sunday mass at Corpus Christi. She was friendly and seemed glad to see him, but something was obviously missing. There was no kidding and no flirting. They talked mostly about the details of their upcoming trips to their schools up north. He had the distinct feeling that she regarded him like an old acquaintance from her past.

Epílogue

October, 1954

TONY WAS STANDING IN LINE TO THE
confessional at the pigeon-stained Polish Catholic church in downtown Wallingford. He was worried. The only thought that cheered
him was that the line was long.

He had been at Choate for only four weeks, but he had already
accumulated a long list of worries. The impending confession for
one. The priest was not going to be too pleased with his list of sins.
He was also worried about surviving his first year at Choate and
did not fully understand why he had to go to a school in Wallingford, Connecticut, 1,500 miles away from Havana.

Wallingford was a horrible little town, a steel mill town. The
tallest building was six stories high, and the town was full of hoods.
The Choate campus, though, was attractive, nestled high up in the

Wallingford hills. Tony knew that Choate was a famous school, the alma mater of more than one U.S. senator. He also knew that he was there because Choate was where the men in his family went— part of the Pasquaney–Choate–Yale tradition his de la Torre grandfather had started. Still, he missed Cuba. He missed the tropics and living close to the ocean. He treasured his memories of his recent summer vacation and wished it hadn't ended the way it did. Even so, up to the very end, it had been a terrific summer. When he heard his new classmates talk about their summer vacation, he thought that what they talked about seemed so silly, so mundane.

But the summer was history, and now at Choate he was worrying about so many things that he did not know where to start. He worried about fitting in; simple things, like whether his clothes stood out as different from the other boys. Choate boys bought their shirts and jackets from Brooks Brothers, and he and his mother, who had brought him to Choate, had bought his clothes at Orbach's. But that was the least of his problems.

His command of English was not as good as he had once thought. He noticed how sometimes he said things that were not intended to be funny, but all his classmates would break out laughing, like the time he had explained to a group of classmates that he was attending Choate because he wanted to go to "jail." Seeing that this statement only elicited some curious stares, he added: "My father and my uncles all went to jail." That second statement seemed to perk them up a little, and there were a few laughs and a loud guffaw. He didn't understand what was so funny about his family's fine educational heritage, but he went on. "Even my grandfather went to jail." Now they were all laughing. It took him a while to learn how to pronounce Yale correctly.

He was also worried that he was not going to live up to the standards set by his father and uncles when it came to sports. He was reminded about his relatives' athletic accomplishments every time he went to the gym and looked at the varsity team pictures displayed on the brick walls. His uncle Miguel had been captain of the baseball team from 1933 to 1936. He was a fine pitcher and had even auditioned for the Yankees. Tony's father, Victor de la Torre, had been captain of the crew team, and another uncle had been the captain of the basketball team. He could recognize the confident smiles of his relatives at the front center of the teams, holding the baseball or the basketball. He also noticed, amused, how his father and uncles seemed to have very large ears.

Tony was certain he was not going to succeed as a football player. He was five feet, three inches, and so thin that his mother took him to doctors. She was afraid that he might have a tapeworm. Everyone on his Choate Peewee team was bigger, stronger and faster. They seemed to know how to play the game, a game he had never played before. The coach suggested he play defensive back, but every time he tried to tackle the runner, the runner ran effortlessly over him. It was embarrassing. Even worse, he was having problems keeping up with some of his classes. The part of his brain that dealt with algebra must have been paralyzed.

He often felt shy with his new classmates, even though he was familiar with American boys thanks to the two summers he spent at Camp Pasquaney. He did notice how the boys at Choate seemed very upbeat and confident, and many were reputed to be extremely wealthy, with names even a Cuban had heard of, like Carnegie and Rockefeller. But Tony didn't feel intimidated. He felt superior to his American classmates in one area; he could tell that most of them had not kissed a girl, and he had done that and more. He had also been in love, and he had already been heartbroken. He was still heartbroken. Cuban boys were much more advanced than American boys when it came to girls.

When he thought about Carmen, he couldn't help but remember how he kissed her at the water's edge. How they held hands for everyone to see on their walk on the beach. And especially, when they danced in the bar at Club Kawama. He thought of that moment as if it had been a scene in a movie, a scene in slow motion; how Carmen had been utterly focused on him, how she focused on him while they danced, oblivious to the world and everyone else. He remembered how he felt; head-over-heels in love. He still couldn't understand how, with such surprising speed, Carmen moved on. She apparently moved on to her next adventure with another boy. He had been just a stepping stone in her romantic history.

Tony also needed to move on, but he couldn't stop thinking about her. He especially thought about her when he played the Cuban records he brought with him. He felt miserable every time he played *La Noche de Anoche*, the song they danced to after he kissed her. Like an idiot, he kept playing that song over and over again in his room. That song was supposed to be their song.

Still, he was discovering this about himself; deep down, he was an optimist. He was thinking that Carmen had been momentarily confused, dazzled by the older boys, by their sophistication, their wit and their cars, but now she might be having second thoughts. First loves are hard to forget. He knew that from his own experience. He had also heard some encouraging news from Tina. She told him that Carmen's infatuation with Robertico Artiaga didn't last long. Robertico's interest in Carmen had apparently lasted one night.

Just to remind her that he was still around, and still thinking about her, he wrote her a letter, describing his experiences at Choate. He was careful to keep everything light and casual. He didn't want to make the mistake of being too honest, a mistake he had made with Sarah's letter, except that on the corner of the envelope of Carmen's letter he wrote: *mailman, mailman, do your duty, and deliver this letter to a Cuban beauty!*

She replied and acknowledged that the mailman thing was funny, but then she only wrote about her school and not much else. He also noticed that his letter was twice as long as her reply. But no matter, he quickly wrote her back. He suspected the worst, that their romance was over, but who could predict the future? They would run into each other again when the next summer vacation came around, in Havana, at the Yacht Club, outside mass and on Varadero Beach. In the meantime, he couldn't help himself. He kept thinking about her. He couldn't accept that she had forgotten their perfect week on Varadero Beach. How could she forget? He couldn't forget.

Still, a few good things were happening at Choate to distract him from his Carmen misery. His English teacher read one of his essays to the class, an account of a fishing trip with his de la Torre grandfather, as an example of good writing. He even said that it was pathetic that de la Torre, a Cuban, was the only one in the class who could spell. The food at lunches and dinners was not bad. A wealthy alumnus had left a fund so that Choate boys could have ice cream for dessert with every meal. Steak or roast beef was served every Saturday. He liked his American roommate, but mostly, he had become very good friends with Emilio; they seemed inseparable.

Emilio was adapting well to Choate; he had made the junior varsity in soccer and was making friends easily. He was also making enemies, due to his penchant for decking his new classmates with a quick right to the chin. It happened first when a much bigger boy, a Southerner named Kittredge, playfully snapped a towel at Emilio's behind in the locker room. Emilio turned around, went up to Kittredge, who was good-naturedly smiling at him, and suddenly clocked him with his lethal right. In that split second, Kittredge must have been really surprised. He was out for three minutes. Word spread fast that Emilio was dangerous.

Tony knew that Emilio was dangerous, but he was more than happy to be his friend. They were spending their free time together, listening to Cuban records in Emilio's room, talking endlessly about Choate, the future and girls. They both planned to go to an American college after Choate and return to Cuba after college. Tony was very sure about that because he wanted to live next to a tropical ocean. Emilio was going to inherit his father's insurance company and wanted Tony to work for him. He wanted Tony to be his vice president. Tony wasn't too sure about that. Selling life insurance sounded like a depressing job, asking prospective clients to give him money so that they could plan for the occasion of their death.

He was starting to feel confident about his future career prospects. During the past summer he had some success with girls. Since girls were amazingly complicated, there was no reason why he couldn't succeed at whatever he decided to do. Besides, everyone knew and respected his de la Torre family in Cuba, and he was going to one of the best American prep schools. He had a leg up on life.

The present, though, did not look promising. There were three or four hours of homework every day. Choate published a weekly assignment sheet for every class, and every class gave homework every day. Even worse, it was becoming clear that they would be living the life of a monk for the next four years. Choate had a clearly defined philosophy of education, and central to it was the idea that the sight or thought of girls was detrimental to the proper pursuit of studies, sports, religion and citizenship. Weeks and months could pass without them even seeing a girl. The only females Choate boys were allowed to come into contact with were the dining room maids, who would not be hired unless they were over sixty and masters' wives, who were mostly unattractive. There was one exception: Mrs. Peterson. She had been a model in New York before she met and married Mr. Peterson. She was still stunningly attractive. She knew it and dressed provocatively. Saturday night dinners at Choate were formal affairs; the boys wore suits and Masters' wives dressed up. There was always a lot of traffic around Mrs. Peterson's table.

But not all was hopeless on the female front. Tony was starting to get excited about a Wallingford girl. He lived in a small house at the edge of the Choate campus. From his window, he and his roommate could see the back of the house where a local family lived. A girl their age lived there, and they could see her bedroom window. She kept her curtains drawn most of the time, but now and then, she opened them. Whenever they caught a glimpse of her, they could tell that she was cute. His roommate had a brilliant idea. They taped a large sign on their window with the message: "Hello. Your name?" She didn't respond at first. One week later she responded with a sign that said: "Betty." Tony decided to be bold. On the next sign he wrote: "Phone Number?" Again, nothing happened for a week. Then a sign appeared with a phone number. Tony called her. He suggested they meet downtown at noon on Saturday. She agreed and suggested they meet at the lunch counter at Woolworth. She said she would bring a girlfriend. Tony said, no problem. He would come with his best friend. The plan was to head for Woolworth after his confession.

The line in front of him was down to a few sinners. He suspected his confession was going to be a disaster. He wasn't even sure why he was confessing his sins. Going to confession on Saturdays had been Emilio's idea, thinking that after going to church, they could explore the town. Catholics were the only students allowed out of the Choate grounds, so they could attend confession on Saturdays and mass on Sundays. Choate had advised its Catholic students to walk downtown in groups, take care of religious business and quickly walk back. Apparently, the townies, all hoods, had one aspiration in life—to beat up a Choatie. Emilio was unconcerned. Tough guys did not scare him. He also claimed he was an atheist, so he would sit in a rear pew and wait for Tony to finish with his confession.

Tony knew he was a terrible Catholic, but for some strange reason, he still felt compelled to go to church on Sundays, out of habit or lethargy. Whatever beliefs the Jesuits had instilled in him were rapidly fading, but he enjoyed the peace and quiet of the one-hour Sunday mass. Mass was his favorite place to daydream—often about girls. He liked the solitude he only could experience in church and the time to let his mind wander without purpose and without interruption. He liked the dark interior of the church, the quiet, the smell of incense, the occasional coughs and how the church environment seemed to trigger elaborate daydreams.

An old Polish looking lady stood in line in front of him. He wondered: what sins could this eighty-year-old great grandmother have committed? He had committed plenty of sins. He had not confessed since Belén, and now he had to include all the sins from his brothel adventures and from summer vacation. He was thinking that an American priest would not understand a Cuban boy's confession.

The Polish lady's turn came. She slowly shuffled forward and painfully knelt down on the padded stool. As soon as she fell to her knees, she pressed her face against the screened window and started an anxious, loudly whispered confession. Whatever she had done, she felt awful about it.

The priest inside the confessional made Tony nervous. His previous Sunday sermon had made an impression: "Imagine a piece of red-hot coal pressed onto the palm of your hand," he suggested. "It would be painful, wouldn't it? Now imagine hundreds of red-hot coals pressed onto every square inch of your body. Think about it. Now, this would be extremely painful, wouldn't it? *Extremely painful*! Now imagine this horrible pain lasting not one second, not ten seconds, but an eternity. *An eternity!*"

It was clear that this priest relished the thought of torment. He hated sinners and wanted them pressed with hot coals. He had a tendency to yell from the pulpit in a booming, disagreeable, European-accented voice. He was old, bald and overweight. He looked evil. He could have played a part in an Inquisition movie. Tony knew this priest would want his god, a vindictive and ruthless god, to roast him like a marshmallow.

The old lady ended her confession and struggled up to her feet. Then, taking tiny steps, walked back to her pew. Tony took a deep breath, moved over to the confessional and knelt down.

"Yes, when was the last time you had confession?"

"Four months ago, Father."

"That is a bit too long, my son. What would you like to confess?"

"Father, I said bad words. I lied. I had bad thoughts."

"Is that it, my son?"

"No, Father."

"Well, what else is there?"

"Father, I masturbated. I got drunk. I saw dirty movies. I French-kissed. I did it with prostitutes."

"*What was that?*" The priest's voice boomed, so loudly that everyone in the church must have heard him.

"What was what, Father?"

"*The last item, young man.*"

"I did it with prostitutes," Tony said, bracing himself.

The priest's head suddenly darted out from the curtained confessional and stared disgustedly at Tony for a good ten seconds. Tony was shocked, convinced that they were not supposed to do that. The priest's head disappeared back into the confessional.

"My son, how old are you?"

"I'm fourteen, Father."

"Fourteen!"

"Yes, Father."

"This is disgraceful!" He yelled again.

"Yes, Father."

"Don't you 'yes, father' me! What do you mean, prostitutes? Did you do it more than once?"

"Yes, Father. Sorry, Father."

"My son, how many times did you commit this terrible sin?"

Tony had to think about that one.

"My son, I asked you a question."

"I'm trying to count, Father."

"You're trying to count!"

"Father, I tried to do it four times, at the beginning of summer vacation, but I only really did it three times."

"My son, is this your idea of how fourteen-year-old Catholic boys should celebrate summer recess?"

"No, Father."

"My son, you have some explaining to do."

"Father, you see, I'm from Cuba. And in Cuba, a confession like this one is normal."

"Normal! This is not normal!"

Tony looked around. The priest's outbursts had not gone unnoticed. All the parishioners sitting nearby were staring at him as if he had leprosy.

"Father," Tony said, in a very low voice, hoping he'd get the hint. "What I mean is, all my friends were doing it, too. My father and all his friends did it at the same age. It's not a big deal. It's a tradition for the boys in our culture. I did it at the Mambo Club, a very elegant place. It has an orchestra."

The orchestra was an exaggeration, but Tony hoped to convey the idea that the Mambo was a classy establishment.

The priest experienced a rare moment of wordlessness.

"My son, this is pitiful, pitiful," the priest finally said. "*I don't want to hear about the orchestra!* This is what I want to know. Are you aware of the enormity of your sins? *Are you aware just how pathetic this confession is?*"

"Yes, Father."

"*But are you repentant?*"

"Yes, Father." Any other answer was unthinkable.

Was he repentant? Truthfully, no. Masturbation was, well, necessary, in order to fall asleep at night. His brothel experiences had been harmless, and he had stopped going and had no plans to go again. The night he kissed Carmen had been a sensational moment in his life, followed closely by his French-kissing sessions with Sarah. Kissing Sarah had a positive effect. It had made leaving Cuba and coming to Choate seem less painful because he could look forward to meeting more American girls.

The priest ignored his response and launched into his favorite description of hell, replete with the burning coals, with the un-imaginable endless pain and informed Tony that it was clear that Hell was going to be his well-deserved eternal destination. The penance was ridiculously long; one hundred Our Fathers and one hundred Hail Mary's.

He walked back to his pew, kept his eyes on the floor and knelt down. After he recited a few Our Fathers, he realized it would take all afternoon to do one hundred, not to mention it would be difficult to keep count. Emilio would be furious, and they wouldn't make it to Woolworth on time. He could imagine Betty and her friend sitting there, waiting for them, feeling disappointed. Besides, doing the penance would be pure hypocrisy.

He suddenly felt comfortable with his next move. He got up and joined Emilio at the back of the church, and they started on the walk up the hill.

It was a windy day, starting to feel cold. The leaves had changed colors and now were flying around. He liked the fall. There was nothing like it in Cuba. He was looking forward to the coming winter, to the first snow and especially, to his first snowball fight. He had already bought ice skates and couldn't wait for the ponds to freeze.

When he thought about it, going to prep school in the United States was not too bad. Where else could he make a connection with a girl by putting up a sign in his bedroom window? Anything was possible in America.

— · —

www.ingramcontent.com/pod-product-compliance
Lightning Source LLC
Chambersburg PA
CBHW051244250626
47155CB00009B/3155